## A Land Without Magic

'Stafford Sparks has escaped from prison!' Hearing that name again was like an icicle piercing Kit's stomach. He had wanted to forget all about that evil magic-hater and his mad ideas to control the world through science . . . Now this . . .

With the arch-criminal Stafford Sparks on the loose again, Kit and his friend Prince Henry could be in terrible danger. So Kit is sent to Paris, out of harm's way, and Prince Henry goes to Callalabasa for the king's coronation. But then Kit learns that Henry's bodyguard is one of the magic-haters and Henry is in even greater danger.

Kit rushes after his friend, determined to protect him, not realizing that in Callalabasa magic is forbidden and the slightest trace of enchantment is punishable by death. How can Kit look after Henry and defeat the evil plans of the magic-haters if he can't use his magic powers? And just why exactly is Callalabasa so important to so many people? Just when all seems lost, help arrives from an unexpected quarter . . .

Stephen Elboz lives in Northamptonshire, and has had a variety of jobs, including being a dustman, a civil servant, and a volunteer on an archaeological dig. He now divides his time between teaching and writing. His first book, *The House of Rats*, won the Smarties Young Judges Prize for the 9–11 age category.

# A Land Without Magic

Other books by Stephen Elboz

Bottle Boy
The Games-Board Map
Ghostlands
A Handful of Magic
The House of Rats
A Store of Secrets
Temmi and the Flying Bears
The Tower at Moonville
A Wild Kind of Magic

# A Land Without Magic

## Stephen Elboz

OXFORD
UNIVERSITY PRESS

# OXFORD

UNIVERSITY PRESS

Great Clarendon Street, Oxford OX2 6DP

Oxford University Press is a department of the University of Oxford.
It furthers the University's objective of excellence in research, scholarship,
and education by publishing worldwide in

Oxford New York

Athens Auckland Bangkok Bogotá Buenos Aires Calcutta
Cape Town Chennai Dar es Salaam Delhi Florence Hong Kong Istanbul
Karachi Kuala Lumpur Madrid Melbourne Mexico City Mumbai
Nairobi Paris São Paulo Shanghai Singapore Taipei Tokyo Toronto Warsaw

and associated companies in Berlin Ibadan

Oxford is a registered trade mark of Oxford University Press
in the UK and in certain other countries

Copyright © Stephen Elboz 2001

The moral rights of the author have been asserted

First published 2001
First published in this paperback edition 2002

British Library Cataloguing in Publication Data available

ISBN 0 19 275199 9

1 3 5 7 9 10 8 6 4 2

Typeset by AFS Image Setters Ltd, Glasgow

Printed in Great Britain by
Cox & Wyman Ltd, Reading, Berkshire

For Marilyn Watts, a writer's friend

Special thanks again to Linda Hitchens who managed to type this *and* pass her driving test

# Prologue

It was a warm, heavy summer's night; over London the moon lay hidden behind towering black clouds, each cloud edged in bright light, drifting slowly along like a lily-pad. In between their passing, the moon broke through in sudden startling bursts, its gleam like wet paint upon the shadows, falling across the various slate roofs, towers, and barred windows of Wormwood Scrubs prison; a forbidding set of buildings even by moonlight, and surrounded by a high brick wall.

To the east thunder rumbled.

Warder Albert Harris heard the thunder and feared it meant a storm brewing. He hoped not—he was not in the best of places if there were, high up on watchtower number three, manning the anti-balloon harpoon gun which guarded the prison from air attack.

By him sat his cat, Nan, flat-eared and bothered by the sluggish heat. Like all other watchtower warders, Harris was a wizard. (Wizards were always chosen for the job.) And each worked closely with his own cat; not any plain ordinary cat either but a specially bred, intelligent, enchanter's cat, which would not run in terror at the first flash of magic. On the towers they were prized for their ability to hear the smallest of sounds; and the prisoners knew they could be as fierce as guard-dogs.

Nan was old, fat, and not particularly clean. She had lost an eye in an alley brawl, yet, battered looks aside, was as alert as any of the younger cats and as sharp as her own claws. She and Harris communicated by mind-walking constantly, each leaving himself open to the other like friendly neighbours who keep their doors ajar.

Thunder rumbled again.

Nan's mind flitted about Harris like a restless moth, before entering and settling.

*Oh, this weather*, she murmured drowsily. *It is so, so hot. Mightn't you do something clever and cool with your magic?*

*Put up with it*, said Harris. *You're a cat and cats should be used to all sorts of weather. If you wanted pampering you shouldn't have become a prison cat.*

He sounded rather short with her, and although Nan put this down to the heat, she rose huffily and drifted back to her own body. A moment or two later, Harris reached down and scratched her ear, then his mind followed as she knew it would. She lay down and closed her eyes.

*There's not even a breath of wind*, said Harris his tone consoling.

She purred.

*No*, she said, *and I have to admit this is one time I wouldn't mind being a human. How pleasant to be able to undo a button or two as you humans can. Fur is such a mixed blessing you know, Albert.*

*Well, I don't think the prison governor would take kindly to me dressing sloppily on the job, even if I am stuck up this blessed tower where no one else can see. And must I keep telling you, cat, it's Mr Harris to you.*

Nan yawned. *Oh, as you like—Mr Harris. But how you humans amuse me with your names and titles. Cats have a far better idea—first win respect with your claws. Be the toughest fighter around and then everyone will call you 'sir' out of natural respect.*

Harris was in no mood to listen to cat lore.

*Kindly pay more attention to your job, cat*, he said. *Is there anything that you hear?*

Nan tilted her head slightly. *Umm . . . mice in the kitchens*, she reported. *Three big ones . . .* She paused, mouth watering. *Plenty of snoring in the cells, of course; one or two prisoners pacing the floor. The odd rattle of chains and the governor's pen scratching on paper.* She yawned again. *Just an ordinary night—*

Suddenly she stopped, and her single good eye glowed amber.

*What is it?* demanded Harris.

*Something in the air.*

*In the air? An airship maybe?*

*I believe so. Over there and heading this way at speed.*

As Harris raced back to his body, she pointed the direction with the tip of her tail, and immediately Harris swung the harpoon gun to face it. He pushed a whistle into his mouth ready if necessary to sound the alarm, and with his thumb casually clicked off the harpoon gun's safety catch.

Nan's mind nuzzled his neck.

*You hear it yet, Albert?*

*No, I'm not a cat—and it's Mr Harris. Now hush up, cat, let me concentrate on my work.*

With his eye fixed to the gun sight he gazed along the barrel out into the darkness. At high points around the prison, blue lanterns flickered out their warning to the city's teeming sky traffic to keep well clear.

Nan rubbed herself against his skull, purring.

*It's getting closer, Albert.*

*So you say. I expect it'll be one of those idiot blimp omnibus drivers. Honestly, these days—half the time they don't bother to look where they are going. Well, if this one thinks he can get away with it without me taking his number and reporting him, he's got another think coming. Now away, Nan, this isn't the time.*

He began to push her out and she leapt from him. She might have been more cross with him had she not been distracted by the snap of a trap and a mouse's dying squeal.

3

Harris stared unblinkingly into the sky.

'There it is,' he muttered at last.

And all at once it was there, the mysterious airship—prow first, unlit—rumbling full-steam out of the dark centre of a cloud and making directly for Harris's tower. Harris's hair prickled and this time not from the heat. Nan drew closer. She spat and her fur stood on end. The airship was charging straight at them like an enraged bull. This was no blimp driver pushing through on a short-cut, this was mischief and no mistake—if not, some madman had been let loose at the controls. Didn't he know he'd be shot down like a toy balloon?

Yet before Warder Harris could blow a single note of warning or drive the harpoon deep into the airship's nose, he dropped upon the platform floor, curled up and whimpering in pain, his hands cupped to his ears. On her back Nan writhed in agony too, her tail lashing back and forth. The airship slowed. From it came a loud, high pitched screech that affected not only Harris and Nan and the other tower-warders and their cats, but everyone in the prison who heard it, jailbirds and prison officers alike; glass rattled and bottles trembled, and several ancient water pipes burst open in a flood of foaming water.

Within a matter of seconds the airship had manoeuvred itself right over the main prison block, and a rope ladder came tumbling down to dangle before a certain window marked out by a blanket hung over its sill. Had anyone been there to notice, anyone not squirming on the ground helpless against the skull-piercing sound, he would have seen the bars at this window being hastily removed (as if cut through beforehand but then set carefully back into place to fool the guards). With the bars completely gone, a figure appeared, struggling through the opening—a big man dressed in an arrowed prison suit, his ears securely muffled.

4

'Boss—boss!'

Through the bars of a lower window a pair of hands waved at him, desperate to catch his attention.

'What about me, boss? You promised to take me with you—remember?'

At last noticing the hands, the tall figure paused midway between stepping from the window-ledge onto the waiting ladder.

'Ah, Bates, I was forgetting . . . ' he said, smiling slyly. 'But then it is so easy to forget you, my dear fellow. Goodbye, I do hope we never meet again.'

The ladder rose with him upon it. Once he was high enough the airship swung round and headed south. Immediately the crippling sound grew less intense.

Head splitting, Harris recovered sufficiently to drag himself up upon his knees, and when he glanced down he saw his old cat lying on her back. Around them came the urgent sound of whistles arising from every other watchtower; while in the searchlight-swept yard below, alarm bells clanged and guards shouted and ran from door to door, bunches of keys rattling at their sides.

For all the great noise and frantic activity, it seemed something might be achieved, but in the end it was a waste of effort. Useless. Prisoner 2541, the most dangerous man in the whole world, had escaped and was already miles away.

In their cells the remaining prisoners signalled their approval, beating their tin mugs against the walls.

The governor, with a hand to his forehead, was on the telephone demanding to be put through to Scotland Yard.

And Warder Harris stood still in his watchtower cradling his beloved cat, endlessly stroking her thick matted fur.

# Chapter One

Alfie smirked and said, 'That sounds like thunder—you sure you didn't do that too, eh, Kit?'

Kit knew Alfie and the rest of the gang were laughing at him. He scowled but couldn't keep it up for long and gradually his scowl slipped into a grin. He supposed he *was* bragging a bit, but then he found it hard not to; after all he *had* spent the entire day at advanced weather control, at which, he might add, he was several levels higher than the others in the gang. Poor Tommy had yet to master a simple snowflake—all he ever got was feathers and slush; while over a month ago Kit had managed to build a complete snowman in the corner of the classroom, giving it the same pointed nose and banana chin as Dr Fogetty the weather-control master: in fact creating such a good likeness that Dr Fogetty had handed out three hundred lines as a punishment, and melted the snowman with a single bad-tempered prod of his wand.

The roll of thunder came again. It was a hot, still night and Kit's heavy school robe clung to him like a well crafted shadow spell. Of course, the roof of the transfiguration hall at Eton Magical Academy at midnight was strictly out of bounds to all pupils with the possible exception of seniors on a star-watch project; but this didn't bother Kit and his gang, quite the opposite. And getting there was always such a thrill, first avoiding the teachers who patrolled the corridors: Dr Cogham, aided by his wily pet fox, Cyril, a creature better at finding stray, out-of-bed wizards and witches than any bloodhound . . . then into the great hall, making sure to hang a muffle charm on the heavy oak door so its creak didn't draw unwanted attention. Once there it was a matter of creeping past the old suits of armour to the chimney, which was wide enough to fly up on their broomsticks—or, in Kit's case, on his flying-carpet—then across the short distance to the transfiguration hall.

They met here regularly, to crib homework or to magic chunks of raw potato into different flavoured sweets. However, most times their main business was to plot what nasty surprises to spring on their teachers during lessons the following day; and tonight was no exception. Apart from Kit there was Tommy, Fin, Alfie, May, and the Betts twins—Gus and Pixie. The only gang member not present was Henry who, as Queen Victoria's favourite grandson, was kept busy elsewhere on royal duties.

Kit tried again to explain his idea for a spell.

'No, I never said I'd magic up a big ol' whirlwind, just one up to here—' He placed a hand against his hip. 'That way it's sure to be fierce enough to blow old Cramps's papers all over the place, and by the time he gets 'em back in the right order the lesson'll be over, so he won't be able to give us no homework. Just think, no incantational grammar for a whole week.'

He beamed at his own cleverness then rocked with laughter at Alfie's more than passable imitation of Dr Cramps.

'Adverbs—adverbs—adverbs, boys,' he said, peering through imaginary spectacles. 'Um—um, where is the poetry in your woeful mumbles?'

'Sounds dang'rous if you ask me,' said May folding her arms. She (like Henry) didn't have a glimmer of magic in her and considered most things to do with enchantment needlessly risky. 'What if you go and blow out all the flamin' windows?'

7

'Wow, hadn't thought of that!' cried Kit, delighted at the possibility and quite misunderstanding May's warning tone. She tutted and raised her eyes.

'Well, I say it's the best idea we've had all night,' said Tommy, chewing on a piece of strawberry flavoured potato—again forgetting what a bellyache it would leave him with in the morning. Alfie and the twins nodded eagerly; Fin didn't react at all, he just kept feeding biscuit crumbs to his pet rat, who in recent months had grown almost as stocky as he was.

'Go on, Fin,' urged Kit, 'admit it's a good idea too. Imagine old Cramps's face—and we can chase around the classroom like mad things, pretending to be helping him catch his papers, but be mixing 'em up even more instead . . . or—or, listen to this everyone, *splashing* the pages with a word changing solution. If we mix it well we can make a certain letter completely disappear, or alter words to say the exact opposite!'

'Yeah!' squealed Tommy, clapping his hands together excitedly.

Fin didn't look up—he pulled a face and shrugged. 'I suppose it's all right,' he said unenthusiastically. 'But we never tried a whirlwind before. Not prop'ly. I still reckon a monsoon spell is better; and the rain'll make the ink run in any case.'

'We done the monsoon spell already,' said Pixie. 'Twice. Besides, most teachers have come to expect it and have a quick-fire umbrella spell up their sleeves in defence.'

Kit narrowed his eyes and wondered if Fin's half-heartedness was because his magic was not as good as his own, and Fin couldn't raise a whirlwind for himself. In that case, thought Kit, he would go ahead and show him how easy it was. Without telling anyone he began the whirlwind incantation, pointing his finger north . . . south

. . . east . . . west . . . calling a breath of wind from each point of the compass.

A gust of strong wind rushed over them, then another from a different direction, and another, and then a fourth, uniting invisibly around Kit who waved his hands and wove them into one with spoken words of magic. And then it took shape—a whirlwind that set their hair and heavy robes flapping.

'Gawd, you want to blow us off this perishing roof?' complained May.

Alfie laughed so much he was more in danger of rolling off the roof because of *that*; however, his laughter soon fell to an uneasy chuckle when the first tiles started to lift and fly through the air, missing his ear by inches; somehow dust and leaves and twigs were sucked into the brew, and the air around them darkened.

Horrified, Kit couldn't understand why the whirlwind was so strong, or why it kept growing—but it did. It had drawn itself up to the size of a Welsh mountain giant and become an unsteady column of spinning air that maliciously chased various shrieking members of the gang from one gable end to the other. Tommy was terrified he'd lose his only pair of spectacles; then his hood blew up over his face and he blundered around, arms waving, gown swirling, until he resembled an unconvincing ghost in a village pantomime.

'Kit, help!' came his muffled wail.

But Kit realized he had lost control over his creation which had grown even larger. To his great shame his power had deserted him and he was left to point a useless finger at the rampaging piece of magic. He didn't know what to do.

Then, in less time than it took to click his fingers, the whirlwind vanished, and vanished completely, not a shred of it remaining. The silence afterwards was eerie; in it a couple of falling tiles were heard shattering distantly on the ground.

'Five hundred lines each,' said a soft yet stern voice. 'You will write: "True enchanters control the wind, only mindless children huff and puff".'

Kit turned suddenly and was shocked to see Mr O'Gloaming, the master of Celtic magic; he was still pointing at the spot where the now vanished whirlwind had been. 'You will have them on my desk by noon this coming Friday, is that perfectly understood?'

'Yes, Mr O'Gloaming,' droned the gang sheepishly, none more sheepish than Kit. The really odd part about Eton, he had learned, was that the teachers never seemed to get upset or angry whenever pupils used magic to play a prank on them. It was as if the teachers expected them to: the tricks kept the teachers on their toes thinking up counter-spells; while it also meant the pupils were all the time sharpening their own magic and cunning. But if a prank went badly wrong—as with the whirlwind—a very dim view of it was taken indeed, since it meant a pupil had over-reached himself; and to over-reach yourself in magic is extremely dangerous.

Ah well, thought Kit, at least it could have been worse, it could have been Dr Cramps. Unlike Cramps, Kit liked Mr O'Gloaming a lot; usually he was a gentle mild-mannered man, slow to anger, who bred little people in old pickle jars; and from the corner of your eye, if you did not look at him directly, you were able to make out shadowy little figures about the size of a sweet pea flower, dancing at his shoulders and pockets.

Mr O'Gloaming pointed and used a few simple enchantments to repair the damaged roof, ducking as tiles flew over him and back into their rightful places.

'Can we help?' offered Pixie meekly.

'Thank you—no, Miss Betts, you and your friends have

10

already done enough,' said Mr O'Gloaming grimly. 'Now back to your dormitories with you and make sure you leave your brooms in the robe room—I shall check later to see that you have. Wait a moment, not you, Kit Stixby. You're to come with me to the Head Mage's study.'

The gang stood and stared at him, open-mouthed in dismay.

'Now?' uttered Kit.

'At once.'

'But that ain't fair, Kit's done nothing worser than the rest of us,' protested Gus.

'*Six* hundred lines,' growled Mr O'Gloaming warningly.

'Don't worry, I'll be fine,' said Kit waving them away. He tried to act unconcerned, but his throat was dry and his voice sounded cracked. To be called to Professor Lamplighter's study was always a serious matter—in the dead of night doubly so. He knew in Professor Lamplighter's room there existed a black book bound in dragon's hide and chained to the wall. It recorded the names of past pupils who had been ex-spelled for outrageous abuses of their powers, which were still only spoken of in whispers. If Kit's name were the next to be written there, he would not only be parted from his gang but from the magic he loved so much. He tried not to think about it; all the same heavy tears brought a tragic gleam to his eyes.

Fin, Pixie, and Gus hovered on their brooms, while May helped Tommy to untangle himself from his gown which had somehow ridden up around his middle; nearby, Alfie was trying all too obviously to attract Kit's attention by mouthing, 'Try to shove a heavy book down the back of your gown,' and miming the actions of a caning master.

'*Seven* hundred lines,' said Mr O'Gloaming, noticing him.

'Gawd, that's practic'ly as long as the Bible,' groaned May. She slid muttering onto Tommy's broom behind him, wriggled herself comfortable and they rose up lightly to follow the others out of sight down the chimney of the great hall, Tommy casting Kit a final mournful glance.

Kit, left alone with Mr O'Gloaming, thought he'd better try to mend matters as well as they would mend. He cleared his throat. 'I'm sorry, sir, truly I am—about the damage and—and for waking you up, of course . . . I suppose the noise of the whirlwind *did* wake you?'

Mr O'Gloaming snapped his fingers and his broom flew obediently into his open hand. 'Not at all, I was up and about in any case—searching for you as it happens.'

Kit was surprised. 'How did you know where to find me?'

For the first time that evening Mr O'Gloaming smiled. 'You may find it difficult to imagine, Kit, but masters were once small boys themselves. In fact many years ago I was a bright young thing right here at Eton.' The smile widened. 'I used to have my favourite after dark places too.'


Professor Lamplighter (nicknamed Old Dry Wicks by his pupils) was the rarely seen Head Mage of Eton School, who in his younger days preferred to ride a cricket bat instead of a broomstick. His study lay in the crooked west tower and was not a place of comfort, being small enough to be lit by a single weak glow-ball, and always smelling powerfully of stale magic. Despite the lack of space, from floor to ceiling along three walls rose shelves of musty old magic books, most of which were centuries old, with many that were rare or priceless—although seeing them made this hard to believe since they were stacked up anyhow, revealing that they were not simply for show but were working books still very much put to use. On the fourth wall, facing the Head Mage's desk, were displayed the wand-canes of Eton's previous Head Mages, each wand-cane mounted on a highly polished wooden shield.

The window had been left open for the benefit of a speedy entrance, and Kit flew in close behind Mr O'Gloaming's broom, dodging his head under the lintel. He was pale and nervous. As he entered, his eyes went straight across to the wand-canes; their names written clearly underneath. He noted a few—

Old Tingler 1699–1712
Wizard Warmer 1719–1724
Thrash and Flash 1797–1819
Stars and Stripes 1840–1861

Some had been used so thoroughly that they were split and frayed.

After the wand-canes the next thing Kit couldn't fail to notice was Professor Lamplighter's bulky form slumped behind his desk, his old silk dressing gown tied up with a living snake that was emerald green and shiny and apparently unconcerned about the knot in its body; while on his head the professor wore a hat like a stocking, the tasselled end resting on his rotund stomach. He must have left his bed especially for me, thought Kit worriedly. Indeed he must have left his bed and been waiting there quite a while because now he had fallen back to sleep, snoring loudly through his thick, untrimmed beard.

Mr O'Gloaming landed first and tapped Professor Lamplighter on the shoulder. He awoke with a volcanic splutter; the snake hissed.

'Sir,' said Mr O'Gloaming, down to business straight away. 'I've brought him to you—Kit Stixby—as requested.'

'Stixby?' mumbled Professor Lamplighter blearily. 'Taught his father, absolutely hopeless at every one of his three R's—runing, riting, and wraith-magic. An utter disgrace to his gown. Once left a troll pup in me wardrobe he did, gave me the fright of me life.'

Kit knew this to be completely untrue, his witch doctor father had never studied at Eton; but he also knew he'd be wise to keep his mouth shut and not interrupt. Professor Lamplighter's craggy red face peered at him across the desk.

'So what do you want, Stixby? If it's to complain about the food—'

'Y-you sent for *me*, sir,' said Kit timidly.

'I did?'

'You did,' agreed Mr O'Gloaming with a firm nod.

Kit saw the old wizard grow momentarily thoughtful, then at last he recalled.

'Ahhh, yes—this arrived while I was tucked away in me bed, minding me own business. Created a devilish racket at the window it did.' He chuckled. 'Thought Jellaby Minor had chucked another curse at me for making him whitewash matron's room after his last failed attempt to blow me up.' He opened a drawer and took out a winged letter, both wings struggling vigorously to flap.

Huffing on his monocle, Professor Lamplighter cleaned the lens on both sides and fixed it to his eye. Kit waited, impatient to know more; his interest had soared the moment he saw the letter had hawk's wings: that made it urgent—ordinary post travelled more slowly by pigeon wing and then only in daylight; while cuckoo-winged letters were for secrets, the message hidden away in a jumble of words.

Unhurriedly Professor Lamplighter held the letter close to his face and reread it slowly to remind himself of what it said. 'Ah yes . . . yes—yes . . . ' he muttered, waggling his little finger in his ear. Finally done he peered over the top at Kit.

'Well, the long and the short of it, Stixby, is this,' he said. 'You are to go to London at once and as quickly as possible. To—' He adjusted his monocle. '—Buckingham Palace.'

# Chapter Two

One of Eton's strictest rules concerned enchanted quills. Quite simply they were forbidden. The reasons are obvious—an enchanted quill might be used to cheat in an exam, or could be made to forge a note in a teacher's writing excusing a pupil from games on a dark, wet, winter's afternoon; enchanted quills had been proven equally as useful in taking the wrist-ache out of writing lines (which the gang thought was the whole purpose of doing them!). But because it was a rule this is not to say it was never done . . .

Arriving back at his dormitory, Kit opened the door and smiled to himself. It was exactly as he pictured it would be: the girls were there of course (which in itself was forbidden) and by the light of a single glow-ball members of the gang stood concentrating their thoughts on a quill apiece, each quill skating elegantly on its nib across its own snow-white piece of parchment, writing— *True enchanters control the wind, only mindless children huff and puff*; while May, who was not able to enchant for herself, kept everyone supplied with freshly dipped, inky quills.

Kit cleared his throat in what he hoped was a teacherly kind of way. It worked beautifully. Every head jerked round at him at once—but seeing Kit beaming at them and not a teacher scowling, the gang was first relieved then clamouring with curiosity.

'Kit, what's happened?' cried Gus as he and the others crowded round.

'What about your quills?' asked Kit teasingly. 'You know the spell curdles if left unwatched. Do you want your lines to turn out in a different language? Welsh, or Greek, or—'

'Blow the quills,' said May. 'Just tell us!'

Already Pixie's quill was scribbling merrily, *Tree anteaters console the worms, oily mink lets chicken hunt puffin.*

Tommy's quill was even more off, dreamily trailing *Trrrrrrrrrrrrr* . . . for over half a page.

Kit flopped down on his bed. He held up the struggling letter by its wing. Alfie seized it first, read it and handed it on. This way it went round to each member of the gang in turn.

'So your dad sent it,' said Pixie frowning. 'Don't say much, do it?'

'But that don't make it any less urgent,' said her brother.

'Says here you need to pack a bag for about a week,' said Fin.

'Yep, that's what I'm doing,' replied Kit. He took out an old carpet-bag from under his bed and into it tossed some clean*ish* vests, pants, and socks, and the three school robes hung up on a bent nail by his bedside. After a few more things he was done, placing his wand carefully on top.

He clicked the bag shut.

'Maybe you're off on holiday,' said Tommy peering intently at the letter through his spectacles and mouthing each word as he read it.

'If I am,' said Kit, 'it's a pretty mysterious way of going about it, and why meet in the middle of the night at Buckingham Palace—is Henry going too? Nah, I can't believe that—my dad hates the idea of me missing any school.'

'Wish I was going on holiday,' said Tommy mournfully. 'Look—'

The gang turned to follow his gaze and groaned. The quills were busy fighting amongst themselves, crossing each other like swords; and one was leaping playfully from parchment to parchment, leaving behind a number of big wet inky blots.

'Why, I do believe you may have to start all over again,' said Kit grinning broadly.


Kit's friends didn't dare leave the dormitory for fear of running into a prowling teacher (or fox) and landing themselves with an extra five hundred lines, so they said their goodbyes to Kit there and then and he slipped away.

Outside, in the dark, shadowy cloister, Mr O'Gloaming waited; Kit, with his flying-carpet under one arm and clutching his bag in his hand, came on him unexpectedly and caught a sudden gleam of movement about his head.

'Oh!'

'Kit, sorry to startle you,' said the master softly. 'Professor Lamplighter asked me to see you safely on your way. In particular he wanted to make sure you received these—'

He held his hand palm down over Kit's head and Kit shuddered as the tingle of magic went through his body right into his bones.

'What was that?' he asked.

'Oh, nothing more than a storm protection spell, plus one or two little charms to guide and speed you on your way. London is a fair distance to travel on your own in the dark.'

'But I'm the best flier in my whole year,' protested Kit fiercely.

'Indeed you are, Kit, indeed you are, but we have our responsibilities towards each pupil.' He studied Kit a moment. 'Have you still no idea why you'd be called up to London at so late an hour?'

Kit shook his head.

Mr O'Gloaming gave him a reassuring smile and patted his shoulder. 'It'll be something and nothing I shouldn't wonder.'

Taking Carpet from beneath Kit's arm Mr O'Gloaming spread it on the ground for him.

'Fly safe now. I hope to be seeing your grubby face back here among us in a few days. Oh, and of course there'll be the endless round of mischief to look forward to.'

'I'll plan summat really special for you,' promised Kit. 'But prob'ly not a whirlwind.'

As he slipped on his goggles and took up his place upon Carpet, Mr O'Gloaming stepped back.

'And don't think by this you've escaped punishment, Kit Stixby,' he called. 'You may write your lines for me on your return—all seven hundred of them. And I'll tell you now, I'm the world's greatest expert at recognizing enchanted writing.'


Riding fast and straight on the crest of Mr O'Gloaming's wind spell, Kit headed to London's first and finest address. All he had about him was the small travelling bag and a headful of buzzing questions. The more he thought about it the more he wondered at the urgency of his summons— the hawk-winged letter, the hastily scrawled message, the request to come straight away . . . Perhaps it concerned Henry. Kit went cold. Had Henry suddenly been taken ill again?

Kit must have been thinking about the matter quite deeply, for when he next checked, he was over some dreary London suburb, trams and steam carriages passing beneath him. On the horizon he saw dry lightning flicker, causing a host of hansom aircabs to reveal themselves as black dots in a briefly silver sky.

Kit barely gave them a second glance; nor did he notice two broomsticks rise from below, follow him for a short distance, then pull up smoothly on either side.

'Kit,' spoke a solemn voice.

'*Father*—' gasped Kit and turning to his other side—'*Aunt Pearl—you too*. This must be really serious.'

'Dear, it possibly is,' she answered. 'But don't slow down, not yet. We'll tell you everything you need to know as soon as we reach the Palace.'

This wasn't good enough for Kit.

'It's Henry, isn't it? I just know that it is,' he blurted out. 'There's something wrong with him, isn't there?'

Aunt Pearl blinked in bewilderment. 'Henry? Why, he was perfectly fine the last time I saw him. Now concentrate on your flying, child. You'll know everything in good time.'

Full of impatience, Kit clutched his bag for the long (to him) five minute ride to Buckingham Palace, spiralling down to land before it on the parade ground. Although very late, Kit was struck by how unusually busy it was, with the guard seemingly doubled. Had war broken out?

'No, Kit, not war,' explained his father as they trod quickly towards the entrance, shadowed like obedient hounds by Carpet and the brooms. 'But I daresay you'll find the news no less shocking.' He paused. 'Stafford Sparks has escaped from prison.'

Kit stopped dead. Hearing that name again—Stafford Sparks—was like an icicle piercing his stomach. He shivered. He had wanted to forget all about that evil magic-hater and his mad ideas to control the world through science; and he believed he had done so when Sparks was put away behind bars. Now this . . .

'But what is that to me?' he asked quietly.

'Lots,' said Aunt Pearl, taking his hand and squeezing it. 'Be brave, dear; remember you were the one mainly responsible for having him put away in the first place. The wretched man may wish his revenge.'

'That's why I've been brought here?'

Aunt Pearl and Dr Stixby nodded. Then Dr Stixby pointed. Above the palace courtyard the royal airbarge—*Flying George*—lay moored. It was not a particularly large airship, but it was very splendid, being entirely silver; at the prow its figurehead was mad King George leaping over a surprised looking sheep, and a lion and a unicorn proudly supported the royal coat of arms upon its upper tail fin. Surrounded by glow-balls the craft shone brilliantly.

At first Kit didn't understand, so his father explained that as Henry was going abroad to attend a coronation, the Queen had generously agreed that for Kit's own safety the flight would be brought forward and he could travel with Henry as far as Paris.

'Paris? *In France?*' Now Kit looked utterly bemused.

'Don't worry, child. In Paris I have a friend,' said Aunt Pearl. 'An old dear friend called Marlow Muir who is an English wizard teaching at the Academy of Greybeards. I have winged him a letter telling him to meet you, so you are expected. You'll be staying with him for a while; and, who knows, it may only turn out to be for a very short time. With the police on his case that Sparks maniac may be recaptured in a day or two, then life can go back to normal.'

She did not sound too convinced, however.

Before Kit could demand to know more, he heard someone call his name, and turning saw Henry bounding over to greet him.

'Glad to see Mr Sparks has not yet got you in his evil power,' he grinned.

Aunt Pearl fanned herself as if made hot at the very idea. 'Now, now, don't even joke about it, Henry. Heaven

21

knows what would happen if ever he got his hands on the poor, dear boy.'

'Prob'ly he'd strap me up to one of his ol' electric machines like he did to Henry,' said Kit, and he demonstrated what he meant by hopping around as if electrocuted, moaning in a zombie-like voice, 'Buzz-buzz-crackle-crackle . . . '

'That boy has a distinctly odd sense of humour that doesn't arise from *my* side of the family,' declared Aunt Pearl disapprovingly. 'Now hurry along through, child, you mustn't keep anyone waiting—especially not the Queen.'

They went into the courtyard.

Kit had never travelled by royal airbarge before and was keen to see inside its flying quarters as revealed through the open doors, each standing atop of a gangway. He saw chairs as grand as miniature thrones, carved tables with glass lamps and cases of stuffed birds upon them, red damask walls, and proper paintings—landscapes and sea battles and the like—which together made the main cabins resemble the noblest rooms in the palace but miraculously squeezed into a much tighter space.

Lots of people milled around outside. Most were crew, of course, dressed in sailor hats, striped vests, white bell-bottomed trousers, and white pumps. The Queen was present too, seated in a chair beside several ladies-in-waiting. Kit saw how she leaned heavily on her stick and kept yawning, but on seeing him she smiled and he returned the smile at once.

'Henry,' he whispered. 'Where's that savage nurse of yours, the one from Yorkshire?'

'Back in Yorkshire I shouldn't wonder,' replied Henry. 'She packed her bags and left in a huff about a month ago. She didn't get along with Dummock, my new manservant.'

He nodded across at a tall thin man, dressed in palace livery, but with extra lace and buttons and bits of embroidery here and there. He stood picking imaginary threads off his sleeve. He had tiny eyes and in Kit's view his nose was far too large for his face. In the way he moved and peered critically at things he was rather like a stork, but the real truth was he was short-sighted enough to need spectacles yet too vain to wear them.

'And who's that behind him?' asked Kit, then motioning towards a figure in a long mackintosh, his narrow-brimmed bowler hat pressed down rather too tightly—almost to the tops of his eyes. Despite the many glow-balls, he held in his hand the most up-to-date and expensive carbon-powered torch Kit had ever seen, and was shining its beam on the different mooring ropes, checking how securely each was tied.

Henry wrinkled up his nose. 'Ernest Skinner, my new bodyguard from Scotland Yard,' he answered indifferently. 'They seem to think I have need of him, especially with Mr Sparks on the loose and, as Grandmama agrees, I'm stuck with him, though if you ask me he's a bit of a cold fish. I doubt he's ever been out of the country before, so what he'll make of Callalabasa is anybody's guess.'

'Where?'

'Callalabasa,' said Henry again. 'It's a tiny place in Eastern Europe.' He laughed. 'Apparently their postage stamps are nearly as big as the country.'

'So why they sending you there?' asked Kit.

Henry shrugged. 'Oh, mother's distantly related to their royal family only she's too ill to go; I'm having to take her place instead. Honestly, Kit, you have no idea how bo-ring coronations are. If the cathedral's not too draughty—which I doubt—I shall probably fall asleep halfway through and start snoring.'

'Think of me then,' said Kit equally as gloomy. 'I'm

being packed off to Paris to stay with some ol' fossil friend of Aunt Pearl.'

They had a mad fit of giggles imagining each other's grinding misery.

Shortly after came the time for take-off: Captain Lamb, a fellow in a spotless white uniform with golden winged epaulettes, his moustache waxed and curled, informed the company that a breeze had sprung up, blowing entirely in their favour. 'Six hours and we should make Pa-ree,' he said rubbing his hands together at the prospect.

One by one with a puff of smoke and a loud spluttering roar the airbarge's engines burst into life. It signalled the moment for last goodbyes, tears (in Aunt Pearl's case) and embarrassing kisses (Aunt Pearl yet again); plus all the little bits of affectionate fussings-over that every youngster has to endure when leaving home and his family—and in this Henry, who was as royal as royal can be, with a grandmother who was Empress over a quarter of the world, was no different to Kit, fussed over by a doting father and an elderly aunt in a ridiculous flowered hat.

' . . . and do be sure to clean your teeth at least twice a day,' Kit overheard the Queen say. 'Your Grandpapa Albert always had such lovely white teeth . . . '

Aunt Pearl pressed a half-crown into Kit's hand and then rushed over to give Henry one too, not realizing they were quite useless once beyond the English Channel. Meanwhile Dr Stixby rolled up Carpet with a point of his finger. It rose and Kit felt it nuzzle itself comfortably beneath his arm.

'Dear me, I nearly forgot the most important thing of all!'

Reaching under his emerald green top hat, Dr Stixby took out what looked like a round chunk of jade threaded onto an ordinary length of string.

'Promise to wear it at all times for me, Kit,' he said.

'It may be a hastily made precaution but it will glow to warn you if ever Sparks is nearby.' He slipped the charm over Kit's head and tucked it beneath his robe. For the first time Kit saw real concern in his eyes.

'Aw, don't worry, Dad, I'll be fine,' he said. He sighed. 'Though I 'spect Aunt Pearl's friend'll turn out as batty as she is.'

'Hush now,' said Dr Stixby smiling, 'she's coming back. She'll be upset to hear you speak that way. Take care, son. I'll send more things in a few days' time.'

A ship's orderly appeared ringing a bell. 'Ladies—gentlemen, passengers please board. Passengers please board . . . final call . . . '

Kit and Henry excitedly hurried up one of the gangways just before it was pushed aside and the airbarge's doors slammed shut and secured. They continued to wave through a porthole, feeling the *Flying George* slip slowly free of its moorings and rise elegantly into the air. At that moment, with most of the crew occupied, Mr Skinner was the only other person in the main cabin with them; he stood further back, hands clenched tightly behind his back, watching.

In a few seconds the Palace had become small, dim and distant, while the rest of London spread out ever wider around it to form a mass of twinkling lights. Then the airbarge's propellers engaged and the *Flying George* ceased to rise and edged smoothly forwards, heading south-east and for France.

Turning, Kit happened to notice Carpet was not on the chair where he had left it—and he saw why. Mr Skinner was making for the door with it, his face showing the same distaste it would have had, had he been arresting an unkempt urchin.

Kit bristled. 'Hey—where you taking my flying-carpet?' he demanded.

Mr Skinner blinked his cold blue eyes at him.

'To the hold, sir,' he said without a flicker of emotion. 'With respect, it *is* rather grubby and we *are* surrounded by so many valuable objects.'

Kit scowled at him, not liking the sound or look of him one little bit. Huh, he might have told him that Carpet was more than three hundred years old—antique three times over—and worth a great deal more than mere gold or silver to any self-respecting witch or wizard; but somehow he felt it was pointless and Mr Skinner would fail to be impressed; besides, Kit sensed the detective was a man who was quietly used to getting his own way.

'Be sure you're careful with it then,' he mumbled.

Mr Skinner said nothing.

When he was gone, Kit blew out his cheeks and said to Henry, 'Well, who does he think he is, eh? You'd think he had summat against magic the way he held poor old Carpet—like it was a month-old kipper left out in the sun. Anyway, he can say what he wants, but Carpet's no more grubby than I am.'

Henry picked a leaf from Kit's unruly hair. 'Hmm, I can see Mr Skinner may have a point,' he grinned.

Despite the *Flying George* having five very fine night cabins for its passengers, each with its own four-poster bed, Henry and Kit decided it was too hot and bothersome to clamber beneath blankets and were much happier to doze on a sofa. Between dozes they awoke to starlight and once to the sudden flash of a lighthouse and the sound of the sea. And each time they did awake they were sure to find Mr Skinner standing perfectly still at the back of the cabin, sweat trickling down from the tight brim of his bowler hat. It was all too unnerving for Henry.

'Doesn't the fellow ever sleep?' he whispered.

'P'rhaps he sleeps with his eyes open like a crocodile,' suggested Kit and they began to snigger until Mr Skinner cleared his throat to remind them he was there and possibly possessed better hearing than they credited him with.

After that, when Kit next awoke it was morning, and glancing through a porthole he caught his first sight of Paris. He knew it was Paris because of its unique docking-towers which overshadowed every other building by far: monstrous, lank, rusting things designed by a Monsieur Eiffel, who single-handedly was responsible for making Paris one of the ugliest cities in the world. Still, seeing one brought a rush of excitement to Kit, and he decided it mightn't be so bad being away from home and school after all.

The *Flying George* moored at an Eiffel docking-tower behind the opera house and was made secure. Outside, on the platform waiting to board, Kit saw a clamouring group of elderly gentlemen, each identical to the next, with elaborate grey whiskers, a top hat, and a sash striped blue, white, and red like the French flag.

'Who are they?' he asked Henry.

Henry groaned. 'Important government officials come to welcome me to France—and do you know how they're going to do it?'

Kit looked on astonished as Henry acted out a sloppy kiss.

'Yuck! Imagine kissing those great hairy faces,' said Kit appalled. 'It'll be like kissing a cartload of grizzly bears.'

'Worse,' said Henry dejectedly. 'At least bears don't reek of week-old tobacco.'

As they watched, the old men began to jostle each other out of the way to be first in line. Several combed their luxuriant beards, others dabbed their lips with handkerchiefs—and one took out his false teeth, polished them on his sleeve, and slipped them back into place again.

Henry shuddered.

Feeling sorry for him and just a little mischievous, Kit suggested an escape.

'How?' asked Henry.

'Easy—come with me. Just be sure old eagle-eyed Skinner don't spot you on the way.'

He led Henry to the hold where Carpet had been flung down in a dark corner behind the trunks. It perked up on hearing its master's voice and rolled open for them to take up their places. Kit pointed and the hold door sprang open.

'*Voila* as they say in France. Now, Henry, your choice. Either a spot of sightseeing or we stay behind and meet a whole heap of scratchy-faced old grizzlies?'

'Anything but the grizzlies!' cried Henry.

An instant later Carpet was sailing through the opening into a patch of sky; the French officials peering over the tower's railings watched it go in dismay; a moment later they were in pursuit, storming the stairs and lifts in an ungentlemanly scramble.

'Prince! Prince!'

Henry pretended not to hear, and Carpet sailed on, weaving an effortless path through a maze of criss-crossing girders, free to drift wherever it liked; Kit lay back with his hands beneath his head, content to let Henry point out the various sights. ('Over there,' said Henry at one time, 'is the place where the French king had his head cut off by the world's first clockwork powered guillotine.')

Lower down the tower, well-dressed Parisians waited to catch aircabs.

'*Vive* Queen Victoria!' someone shouted, at which everyone applauded politely.

Then Carpet landed, and scarcely had it touched firm ground than Mr Skinner was rushing up, his face black with fury.

'How *dare you* be so thoughtless and irresponsible,' he raged at Kit, immediately attracting a crowd of curious onlookers. 'What if the prince had fallen? What if he had been killed? Had you given a single thought to that? No— but let me tell you this, if he had come to any harm it would have been entirely your fault—you stupid, stupid, selfish boy!'

'Stupid yourself!' returned Kit, no less angry than the detective. 'Henry's my best friend, I'd never hurt him. And for your information he's ridden on Carpet hundreds o' times before now and nothin' bad has ever happened—it never will, because I'd protect him with my magic!'

Mr Skinner stiffened and his voice grew icy. 'May I remind you that it is my job to see to the prince's safety at every hour of the day. I will not have him needlessly put at risk by anyone. And,' he added sneeringly, 'as to the worth of your *magic*, I would not like to say.'

Then, before anything more could be said—even a simple goodbye—Mr Skinner threw down Kit's bag and swept Henry away, muttering, 'This way, sir, I believe some important French gents are keen to meet you.'

Slowly the crowd lost interest and began to move away, drifting around Kit who was too wrapped up in his own fury to notice, wild and dangerous sparks dancing at the corners of his eyes.

He blinked only when a shadow crossed his face.

'Pearl was right,' said a voice. 'She said you had a temper hot enough to make a band of hobgoblins turn and run. Ah, and as I look about me what do I see? Not a single hobgoblin in sight in all of Paris . . . Yes, she was certainly right, your aunt.'

Taking notice, Kit saw a comfortable lived-in face, from the chin and jowls of which hung a long wispy beard.

The wizard held out a hand stained with cabbage-bug juice. 'Professor Marlow Muir,' he said winking an eye. 'You can only be young Master Stixby.'

# Chapter Three

'I can tell you are still angry, you keep crackling your
magic around your mouth which is a sure sign, and
which to some is as irritating as grinding teeth, but
I don't mind in the slightest. Crackle on as much as you
want, dear boy.'

Kit realized Professor Muir was right, he was *crackling*.
As they walked across to the professor's broomstick
propped against the foot of the tower, he had hardly paid
any attention to the friendly old wizard beside him or the
unfamiliar sights all around. This should be as good as a
holiday, yet here he was eaten up by angry thoughts about
Mr Skinner.

He threw a sly glance sideways at the professor and
was surprised to hear him say, 'Stop and take a proper
look if you would find it more convenient; I have looked
*you* over as much as I mean to—dark eyes, unruly hair,
grubby nails—'

Kit quickly slid his hands beneath the bundle of Carpet.
Professor Muir smiled.

'—which I always consider a reliable sign of a good
honest wizard.'

Kit smiled too. He liked Professor Muir: he had a way of
speaking that made everything sound important or wise. So
Kit stopped and looked him up and down as the professor
had invited him to, which some (Aunt Pearl at the top of the
list) would believe a terrible lapse of manners—Professor
Muir, however, only beamed agreeably.

He held out his arms in a gesture of hopelessness.

'See, just a plain, straightforward, much patched, dog-eared, old English wizard—I'm afraid those stylish French gowns have quite passed me by.'

'You'll do,' said Kit with a firm nod of his head.

'Good, then we approve of each other.'

They continued walking a little longer until they reached the professor's broom.

'Are you still thinking about that man—what is his name? Mr Skinner?'

'Umm . . . a bit,' admitted Kit. 'I don't think he ever liked me right from the start—and d'you know, I think he didn't like me as soon as he saw I was a wizard.'

'Ah,' said the professor suddenly interested. 'Let me tell you, Kit, there exists in our world a number of people who despise magic whatever form it takes. These people have been amongst us since the beginning of time and most will give their reasons for their hatred, but usually it boils down to two things. Jealousy and fear. You must be aware of this yourself—Stafford Sparks couldn't be a better example . . . and I should be aware of it too. It is my work at the academy to record and study in depth some of history's most toe-curlingly nasty magic-haters.'

'Really?' said Kit impressed.

Professor Muir nodded. 'Now have you a burning desire to learn more on the subject or shall we proceed to the academy?'

Kit shook his head. 'No, but how I really wish I'd magicked a boil on Mr Skinner's nose . . . or . . . or a place he only finds out about when he goes to sit down!'

Professor Muir chuckled. 'Then it is as well a wizard's magic ebbs in anger, or think how afterwards we may regret it.'

They flew to the Academy of Greybeards which stood very close to the Sorbonne. On the way Kit marvelled at the recklessness of French blimp drivers, who drove at breakneck speeds, not caring if they bounced into each other, and blaring their klaxons at every opportunity. Kit was glad to keep his distance.

One short but scary journey later they put down in a courtyard strikingly designed to look like four cliff faces coming together, with doors and windows made to resemble caves and crevices, and gargoyles perched on top not unlike their English cousins back home on St Paul's (but none as wonderful as Balthasar, Kit's favourite gargoyle in the whole world). Upon craggy balconies, Kit observed French professors of magic, pacing up and down in their elegant grey cashmere robes, some smoking heavily, others muttering and waving their arms as if holding an argument with themselves. They all looked anguished and lost in thought.

Professor Muir raised his eyes. 'Ah, these clever French chaps,' he said. 'They talk about magic, they think and dream about magic, they wonder why we have it and what it really is, but few practise it. I bet between them they couldn't organize themselves together to boil an egg. They've gone and forgotten h—'

He stopped suddenly, distracted by the violent slamming of a wide green door within a porch of pretend stalactites; on the top step before it stood a dumpy, red-faced woman, a packed case upon either side. She buttoned up her coat over her apron.

'Hmmph!' she snorted giving a very final shrug.

'Oh dear, do I detect trouble at camp,' murmured Professor Muir. 'Madame Lavette,' he called. 'Nothing wrong, I trust?'

'Wrong? Wrong? The whole world go wrong, Professor *Moor*. It go crazy!' Her eyes flashed angrily.

She advanced, bumping Kit aside with one of her suitcases as if he didn't exist. Flinging them down she thrust a large front door key into Professor Muir's hand.

'It no good!' she cried. 'I leave. I housekeep for you no more, Professor, that *thing*, that evil little monster, he escape again. He destroy my kitchen—crash-pow!—he throw plates at my head—he try to bite me! He stay—I go. *Au revoir!*'

With that she picked up her luggage and stormed off muttering strong French all the way.

'Ah.' Professor Muir pressed his fingertips together before his mouth. 'From that I may safely deduce that Luddite has escaped once more.'

'Luddite?' said Kit curiously.

'My gremlin*,' explained the professor. 'A few weeks ago I had need to raise one for my experiments, so I crossed a marmoset monkey with a sextant. Knew at the time there was too much brass in his character. Even so I developed such a soft spot for the little devil that afterwards I hadn't the heart to change him back; and now it seems he is on the rampage. Poor Madame Lavette.'

From deep inside the building a crash arose. The professor turned appealingly to Kit.

'Will it be too much of a nuisance if I asked you to help me catch him?'

'Jus' try stopping me,' replied Kit, feeling his magic swell at the prospect of a gremlin hunt.

Careful not to make a noise they crept into the professor's hallway, setting aside broom and carpet; Kit put down his bag and stood surveying the damage. A once

*Any creature created when an animal is magically crossed with a machine. Gremlins come in many forms, but are usually small, strong, and very fierce. All share a deep dislike of humans and things mechanical. Gremlins are classed Grade 2 in the lists of dangerous creatures because of their extremely destructive nature. *Encyclopaedia Magica*, 1851 edition.

34

rather handsome atmospheric clock lay smashed across the tiles—

'Oh dear,' said the professor covering his mouth.

—several mangled parts from a tide forecaster glittered at the bottom of the stairs—

'Oh dear, dear, dear.'

—and an antique spectrephone used in communicating with ghosts lay shattered against the wall, as dead now as the things whose voices once came crackling from its receiver.

'Oh dear, dear, dear, dear, *dear* . . . This is far worse than I expected.'

'I once had a pet lizard a bit like this,' said Kit, trying to make the professor feel a little better. 'It chewed through everything it did. In the end I gave it to my pal Alfie and it chewed through the toes of his father's boots . . . Dunno what happened to it after that—'

A crash and the urgent scampering of paws caused all thoughts of lizards and chewed boots to vanish.

'It's up there,' said Kit lowering his voice and squinting up the stairway. 'Let me go, Professor, I'm good at tracking animals; and if I can't catch it I'll drive it down to you.'

Before Professor Muir could come up with a better idea or a reason not to, Kit sprang forward, broken glass crunching underfoot, and leapt up the stairs three at a time.

At the top he discovered a landing with four closed doors, unremarkable except for their handles which were living hands. Three were waving madly in an effort to attract his attention, and when they had it they pointed all together at the fourth door, where a badly scratched hand hung limp as if in shock. Kit crossed to it and held it in his own hand. The poor thing trembled. Then it revived, shook Kit's hand vigorously as if to wish him good luck and, as the door opened, patted his back and propelled him a few steps forward.

'All right—don't push,' hissed Kit.

Using the door as a shield, Kit peered cautiously around it, hearing fretful grunts and growls arising from the other side, and seeing a small magic laboratory like the ones they had at Eton, only much better equipped and without the graffiti.

Opening the door a little more he suddenly caught a movement and *then* he saw it—the gremlin—the very first gremlin he had ever seen.

Like a tiny bad-tempered god, Luddite squatted on a fiery sun in the centre of a model of the solar system. In one paw he gripped Mars, in the other Saturn, and at that moment he was biting each planet in turn, spitting out broken pieces like pips.

Studying the gremlin more closely, Kit had to admit he had never before seen a creature quite so strange. His fur was thick and coarse and rose in wiry tufts at his ears, which was hardly surprising since this was what it was—tufts of wire, copper wire; while on his chest the resemblance was closer to metal shavings from steel or silver. He had a long thick tail more like a cable than anything else, fraying at the end; and cogs where knee and elbow joints are usually the rule. He had brass claws and brass teeth, eyes like dark pools of mercury, and possibly the angriest expression Kit had ever seen on a creature so small.

All at once the gremlin paused, raising his head to sniff the air. His sharp snout sensed Kit a moment too soon. For as Kit sprang out from behind the door, the gremlin leapt high. A jagged branch of magic shot from Kit's hand, but instead of stunning the gremlin as he had hoped, it merely left half a dozen planets dented and smouldering on the floor. Luddite fled into the next room with a frightened screech.

'Stars' teeth!' cursed Kit and followed.

From the laboratory an archway led straight into the professor's library. With no way out, not even a window, Luddite paced restlessly along the shelves, throwing down books and chattering angrily. Kit ran in and a well aimed volume bounced off his head.

'Ow! That hurt!'

Luddite rose up on his hind legs and screamed, throwing as many books as he could lay paws on. They thudded down. Dodging from side to side, Kit had to admire his spirit, but enough was enough.

He pointed again . . . unwisely as it happened. Appearing out of nowhere, a heavy black book on the nature of bad luck struck his wrist and knocked his hand aside. A flare of magic fuelled by surprise and annoyance left him as a hurtling ball of raw power. It struck the shelves exploding books and papers into the air and knocking a considerable lump of plaster off the wall. More shelves and books came crashing down with it. Shocked into stillness, Kit stood with torn pages and curls of burning ash fluttering down around him.

Only Luddite had the wits to seize the moment. Fur on end and hissing, he streaked along the bookcase and dived from the room. A few seconds later Professor Muir dashed in; he viewed the smoking ruins with horror.

'My library!' he gasped.

'I'm s-sorry.' stammered Kit. 'It was a horrible mistake—it all sort of happened before I could stop it and . . . and . . . '

Professor Muir sank down onto a heap of books, twiddling his fingers through his beard, his eyes flittering restlessly from broken book to broken book. He touched a charred shelf and a few more volumes came tumbling down.

Kit winced, it just kept on getting worse. Then after a few moments he heard the professor speak.

'No, Kit, you are not to blame. I'm the one entirely at fault here,' he said sadly.

'But—'

He held up his hand, silencing Kit's protest. 'I should have reverse magicked that ungrateful creature when I had the chance.' He smiled wryly. 'As your dear Aunt Pearl is fond of saying, ''Be prepared for broken china if you bring a gremlin into the world''.'

Huh, sounds a typical Aunt Pearl type thing to say, thought Kit; and looking round he said, 'Where did it shoot off to?'

'Who—Luddite? Heaven knows, but I sincerely hope you've scared him away and I never set eyes on him again—or any of his kind. I promise on my beard that from this day forth I am finished with gremlins for ever.'

Using magic and dustpans and brushes, they did their best to restore the library to how it was before, but much of the damage was way beyond patching-up or repair. When he realized this, Kit couldn't be busy enough on Professor Muir's behalf; he felt so miserable and guilty. He wondered if he might have felt better had the professor lost his temper and shouted at him, but the old wizard remained remarkably calm and philosophical.

As Kit closed up books and tidied away papers, he saw they mostly dealt with Professor Muir's interest in magic-haters. Not at all pleasant reading for a young wizard. And there glaring up at him were Matthew Hopkins and John Stearne, the infamous seventeenth-century witchfinder generals, who tracked down and put to death many poor innocent witches who probably did nothing more harmful than make and sell a few simple charms. Alongside the old and ancient were also the present day haters; and tucked away amongst the loose sheets Kit found newspaper clippings from around the world.

Then something caught his eye. He gasped and pulled it from the pile to study it more closely. It was a cutting from a recent newspaper (leastways it was not yet yellow): an article about magic, with a photograph. The writing was half burned away, the photograph untouched; and it was this which had first caught and now fixed Kit's entire attention. It showed a group of men who at first glance appeared to be wearing grand-wizards' ceremonial robes . . . only on looking a little harder the magical symbols upon them were either upside down or distorted into mockery.

'Professor—Professor, what is this?' he said showing the photograph to the wizard.

He took it and frowned. 'That, Kit, is something to be wary of. The Knights of the League against Magic. They have very little time for the likes of you and me, I'm afraid. Why does it interest you so much?'

'There!' Kit jabbed down his finger upon one of the faces in the back row. 'Don't you recognize him?'

Professor Muir held the paper closer to his nose. 'Without my proper reading spectacles—'

'Skinner!' shouted Kit excitedly. 'Ernest Skinner. No wonder he didn't like me. The man is a fully paid-up magic-hater!'

# Chapter Four

After the library the rest of the house needed putting back in order, the gremlin having been extremely keen to show his contempt for humans and on a grand scale. Kit did what he could, this time feeling less responsible for the damage . . . but then he did have other matters on his mind.

By early afternoon, with the sun streaming in through the opened french windows of Professor Muir's living room, they fell back into a comfortable armchair apiece, tired and hungry. Without Madame Lavette, his housekeeper, the professor had done his best to rustle up something to eat and drink. There were crumpets (flown over each week on the Fortnum and Mason airship), and some squashed cream cakes (Kit avoided the one with the gremlin paw-print in the middle), and tea (Professor Muir was an English wizard after all!). The teapot's spout had been broken by the gremlin and patched with magic, yet tea managed to dribble everywhere. Clattering his plate and spilling sugar, Kit grabbed and chomped and slurped, manners appearing optional.

'Now, where were we . . . ? The Knights of the League against Magic,' said Professor Muir out of nowhere.

Kit paused in licking his knife and gawped at him. How did he know what he was thinking—could the professor mind-walk into his head without his knowing? Briefly, to test his theory, Kit thought of something extremely rude involving the professor's beard, a goat, and something smelly usually found in a farmyard. The professor did not flinch so Kit knew for certain he was alone in his own head. That, or the professor was a first-rate actor.

'Nasty bunch of individuals if ever there was,' continued the professor, pouring tea and frowning at the spillage. 'Some quite rich and well connected; after all, who says you have to be a penniless unknown to be a magic-hater.'

'So what sort of things do they do?' asked Kit.

'Do . . . ? Well, for a start they hold rallies and publish outrageous leaflets claiming that magic is an uncontrollable danger; that it corrupts all decent minded folk who come into contact with it. Rubbish like that. Secretly they're involved in more unsavoury business. I know for a fact they've tried to blow up the homes of several important wizards and witches.'

Kit picked a crumb off his cake and chewed it thoughtfully. 'Don't the police try and stop 'em?'

'Not yet, the League is too cunning. But they would certainly be interested in Mr Skinner. Why, a magic-hating bodyguard to a prince whose best friend is a wizard, and whose family—his grandmother in particular—is so openly warm towards enchanters . . . No, I suspect Scotland Yard knows nothing of Mr Skinner's links with the League.'

'And Henry?' asked Kit anxiously. 'What about Henry? Do you think he may be in some sort of danger from Mr Skinner?'

Professor Muir did not answer in a direct way. 'The League contains some very unpleasant people,' he said meaningfully.

For a moment there was silence. Then Professor Muir turned abruptly to Kit.

'Naturally you have every intention of flying after the royal airbarge to warn your young friend,' he said, again echoing Kit's exact thoughts. 'No doubt you are also eager to learn the precise hour at which I go to bed so you can sneak away under cover of darkness.'

'You won't be able to stop me,' said Kit fiercely. 'You'd have to lock me in a magic-proof dungeon first.'

'I could fly with you.'

'No!' Kit was very firm. 'No offence, Professor Muir, but you ride your broom like my Aunt Pearl.'

'Carefully?'

'*Slowly*.'

The professor was amused. 'What about your flying-carpet? There's plenty of room on that for two.'

Kit shook his head. 'You'd still slow me down, the extra weight, you know . . . And Henry's three, maybe four hours ahead of me already.'

'Then you must do what you have to, alone,' said the professor quietly. 'Go now before it gets dark and you lose any more time.'

Kit stared at him. The professor was unlike any other grown-up he had ever met, yet still he could not quite believe it.

'On my own? You mean it? Go after Henry all by myself and tell him exactly the kind of person Ernest Skinner really is?'

Professor Muir nodded. 'Yes, I can't stop you or travel with you; you will go in any case whatever I say or do, and I'd much rather you flew across Paris in the daylight so you can see those crazy French blimp drivers hurtling straight at you.' He smiled. 'Another crumpet before you go . . . ?'

Kit was at a loss for words, but he decided there and then that when he grew up he wanted to be exactly like Professor Muir.

* * *

42

Outside in the courtyard Kit spread Carpet on the grass, pulled on his goggles, and climbed aboard.

'Don't forget this,' said Professor Muir handing him his bag.

Kit smiled his thanks and scanned the skies. Bright, blue, and cloudless: perfect flying conditions, he thought—the question was, flying where?

He knelt forward and spoke to Carpet.

'Listen, Carpet, I know what I'm asking is difficult, only please try your hardest. I need to find Henry, he's on the *Flying George* somewhere between here and Callalabasa. Sorry I can't be more precise. I know it's a big sky and a long way, but if any flying-carpet can track him down it's going to be you, you're the best flying-carpet in the whole world.'

Under him he felt Carpet stir with pride and had just enough time to shout his goodbyes to the professor before it shot up vertically, steadied a moment then leapt forward, zooming low over the rooftops. Blimps and aircabs went by in a blur; as did spires, domes, and Eiffel towers. In a few minutes the city had gone.

Good ol' Carpet, thought Kit as he gazed down at the peaceful countryside. Over rivers they flew, over farms, over quaint little villages; over lanes and bridges and haymakers who pointed up at them, straightening their aching backs. Yet when Kit started to recognize some of the features, he knew that Carpet was struggling to keep on Henry's trail and was doubling back in order to find it again. Slowly the sun went down, shadows lengthened. It grew dark . . . then darker. Then it turned cold.

With nothing to keep him warm, Kit put down in a field of cabbages and robbed a scarecrow of its coat.

'*Merci, monsieur,*' he said, giving an elegant bow as he imagined an old-fashioned highwayman doing, then he sniffed and pulled a face. The coat smelt worse than the cabbages; in one of the pockets he found an old bird's nest; and the whole thing was so long and stiff that its hem scraped along the ground. Still, it was better than shivering with cold . . . he supposed; and he was in no position to be choosy.

With his beggarly coat done up where buttons remained to be done up, he set off on Carpet again, this time blessed with stars to guide them. And, as they flew, the land became more and more hilly, with remote farms, and villages tucked away in narrow valleys, and sheep and goats on the hilltops nibbling bracken.

Kit watched the sky as keenly as any cloud-clipper captain, until finally he spied something that made him push up his goggles and focus all his attention on it. It was a string of yellow lights skirting a great cloud. Carpet banked hard and with its fringe rippling, streaked towards it—its bright patterns glowing with confidence.

'Is that it, Carpet?' whispered Kit excitedly. 'Is that the *Flying George?*'

He hoped it was, his fingers were nearly numb with cold. Quickly the travelling airship took shape, although it hardly appeared to move at all, set in the vastness of the night sky. Starlight made it shine; Kit kept his eyes fixed to its upper fin. He couldn't be sure, but . . . yes, there it was—lion, unicorn, the shield between—*the royal coat of arms.*

'Oh well done, Carpet,' he blurted out. 'I'd give you the hug you deserve but I'd prob'ly fall off. Now go closer for me and pull up alongside the hold door. With any luck no one will have locked it again after me and Henry made our escape through it back in Paris.'

The hold door was right behind the rear starboard propeller, the noise and turbulence were awful. An exhaust funnel blew thick choking smoke into Kit's face and he felt soot brush his skin like black snowflakes.

44

'Steady, Carpet, take me up as close as you can.'

Kit knew he was inches away from being finely shredded by the roaring propeller; Carpet rode the rough wind like a swimming snake.

Carefully—very carefully—Kit reached out for the handle. His unfeeling fingers curled around it and he pulled hard. The hold's heavy outer door flew open and Kit laughed aloud at the ease with which Carpet was then able to complete the business, slipping sideways into the opening. Once inside, Kit quickly fell silent, jumping down and rushing across to pull the door to.

No sooner was it shut than he was forced to leap for cover behind a stack of wooden trunks, pulling Carpet and his bag with him—someone was coming, alerted no doubt by the noise.

The inner door opened and a figure stepped in, calling back over his shoulder. 'No, I'll see to it. I expect one of the trunks has worked loose and fallen down.'

Kit kept perfectly still. It was Mr Skinner.

An electric light clicked on. Kit squinted up his eyes, finding it unexpectedly harsh after the velvety grey glow of the stars.

'Seems to be in order,' he heard the detective mutter.

Good job, thought Kit. Then he waited for the light to go out and for Mr Skinner to leave but, as the minutes passed, neither happened. Why can't he just go, wondered Kit, caught in the agony of waiting. He wondered if Mr Skinner had spotted something and was cruelly playing cat and mouse with him (Kit the trapped mouse in the corner).

Or was there another reason?

Daring to take a chance, Kit peered out and saw Mr Skinner gazing through a narrow gap at the inner door, as if making sure no one was around to disturb him. The detective took his time about it but when finally satisfied, he closed the door and crossed to a leather box and unlocked it. The front came down and Kit saw a valved wireless set, the type used for transmitting and receiving messages.

Mr Skinner put on a pair of earphones and clicked down some switches; it took a further minute before the valves began to glow. The machine crackled into life.

Mr Skinner raised a speaking-tube to his mouth.

'Wolf to pack—wolf to pack—transmitting. Are you receiving me? Shall I proceed?'

Kit saw the valves flicker, but anything said in reply was lost to him, heard only by Mr Skinner in his earphones.

'Yes . . . nicely back on course,' said the detective. 'Sticky moment there in Paris though, that wizard kid drawing attention to himself with his flashy magic . . . Yes, worried me too. He should never have been allowed on this voyage in the first place—it's too important to us . . . Ah well, at least he's gone now and there's not a trace of magic left on board. I can't tell you how relieved I am at that . . . Very well, I'll contact you once we reach Callalabasa—at the back of beyond.'

He flicked several switches and the valves began to cool. The speaking tube and earphones were carefully coiled into place and the leather box was closed and locked. Then straightening his bowler hat and whistling jauntily, Mr Skinner stepped from the hold and was gone.

Kit found he was chewing his bottom lip. For him the wireless set and message only confirmed what he already believed, that Mr Skinner was up to no good—and with him in this were others. Thinking about it, Kit wondered if 'wolf pack' wasn't a code name for the League, the detective's fellow cronies against magic. Whichever way Kit looked at it, it was all beginning to add up to something rather worrying; inside him his magic simmered down to a low dispirited flame.

46

Part of the problem was he felt so frustrated at not being able to tell anyone; for not wishing to run into Mr Skinner he had already decided to remain where he was until sure most of the ship was asleep. Then—and only then— would he creep out and make his way to Henry's cabin. It meant passing an uncomfortable few hours in the darkened hold but, as he told himself with grim humour, better a sore back than a knife in it!

He pulled Carpet and the scarecrow's old coat tightly about him and snoozed a shallow unrewarding sleep, for the hold's floor wasn't exactly soft, nor were the walls soundproof, the noise from the engines soon giving him a pounding headache.

By the time he was ready to move, his joints were stiff and his back hurt as much as his head, and he was very cold.

'Come on, Carpet, I'll make sure you're well hidden first,' he said, bending down like a creaky old man.

Carefully he concealed Carpet beneath his discarded coat. This done, he slipped from the hold into an empty corridor, the noise from the engines gone in the closing of a door. Before him the electric wall lamps glowed very low, the weak light reflected on the opposite side by a row of brass door knobs; but as dim as it was, there was more than enough light for Kit's purposes coming after the total blackness of the hold. He counted along, Henry's door fourth and last in line.

He crept towards it, his footsteps muffled by thick carpet and his breath held in check . . . Almost there. Yet even as his hand reached out for Henry's door, the neighbouring door violently burst open and before Kit could do anything an arm locked tightly around his neck.

Strong hands spun him around. His head was forced up. He found himself face to face with Mr Skinner, seeing his mouth drop open. And, at that moment, it was hard to judge who was the most surprised.

Roused from his bed and 'urgently requested' to come to the main cabin, Henry sat in his yellow silk pyjamas and dressing gown, barely half awake and yawning deeply. Before him on one side stood Kit, hot and angry, and on the other, Mr Skinner, cool and watchful. It was all too confusing at this hour of the morning.

'I tell you, Henry, this man is a magic-hater who is up to summat and prob'ly summat very nasty,' said Kit loudly (his throat and neck still red). 'I saw his photograph in a newspaper—he belongs to a bunch called the Knights of the League against Magic.' For emphasis Kit thought this worth saying again. '*Against magic*, Henry. Just you think about it. They're against me for nothing more than being a wizard, and they're against you for being my friend.'

'Can I see?' said Henry interrupting him.

'What?'

'This newspaper with Mr Skinner's photograph in it. Can I see?'

Kit's face reddened. 'Well . . . I don't happen to have it on me, not at the moment . . . ' Unexpectedly thrown on the defensive, Kit felt annoyed that Henry of all people should doubt his word; while it made his blood boil to have Mr Skinner turn to him with that self-satisfied smirk on his face.

'How convenient,' he murmured.

'Do you admit it was you I saw?' challenged Kit furiously.

'No I do not, there must be hundreds of people who resemble me in some way; and photographs in newspapers, well, they hardly give a flattering likeness to anyone. I say you are mistaken.'

48

'And *I* say *you* are a magic-hater up to summat you shouldn't,' cried Kit and he turned appealingly to Henry. 'You saw how mad he got when I let you have a ride on Carpet, didn't you, Henry? That's because it's magic. And he hates magic. And what about his secret wireless message to his *friends*, ask him about that, eh, Henry.'

Henry yawned. 'Well, Mr Skinner?'

'Secret?' answered Mr Skinner. 'Hardly that, sir.' He smiled and Kit felt it was almost a game to him. 'Your young companion merely overheard me reporting back on our progress, that is all.'

'I heard you gloating because I wasn't on board. You were glad I was gone because of my magic. Deny that if you can.'

'Not *gloating*—but I will say I was pleased.'

'Oh, Mr Skinner, why was that?' asked Henry.

Mr Skinner turned to him. 'Because, sir, Callalabasa to which we now fly—to which you go as an honoured guest for the coronation of its new king—is a country where magic is absolutely forbidden. That is the reason I was extremely relieved not to have a wizard aboard, I was thinking of how it might look.'

By now Henry had heard enough. 'There, Kit, everything fully explained, so can I *please* go back to my bed?'

Kit didn't answer, he was still reeling from the shock of Mr Skinner's words. 'What . . . no magic in the whole country?' he said quietly. 'None at all?'

'None,' replied Mr Skinner sharply. 'The smallest charm will see you thrown into their deepest dungeon.' He turned to Henry. 'I daresay we shan't lose too much time, sir, if we put down to let your friend off.'

'Can't do that, Mr Skinner, take a look out of the porthole,' said Henry. 'Those are the Alps, aren't they?

49

I'm not leaving Kit on top of a mountain to fend for himself . . . He'll just have to come along with us.'

'But—but Callalabasa, sir, and its law—'

'Pooh, such a silly law to have in the first place,' declared Henry dismissively. 'Besides, if Kit pretends he isn't a wizard and sits on his hands instead of doing magic with them, who'll be any the wiser? I'll get Dummock to sort him out some ordinary clothes in the morning, he always packs far too much in any case. Tell me, Kit, how do you feel about wearing trousers again—will it be *too* terrible for words?'

Kit smiled. 'Pure torture, though I 'spect I'll survive.'

'And there can be no more magic till we return to England.'

Kit nodded. 'Trousers and no magic it is.'

'I must speak out, sir, I'm far from happy about this,' said Mr Skinner stiffly.

'Speak out all you wish, Mr Skinner, I'm altogether too sleepy to listen to a single word. G'night to you both.'

Yawning, Henry drifted off back to his cabin.

When he was gone, Mr Skinner faced Kit, his eyes metal cold.

'Watch your step, boy,' he said in a threatening growl. 'Just watch your step. Because I shall be there watching you every inch along the way, waiting for you to trip up and land on your face. Remember that.'

His expression hard and grim, he marched off down the corridor. Kit stuck out his tongue.

'There, smarty, you didn't see that,' he said. 'And don't worry about watching me, Mr Skinner, *I* shall be busy keeping my beady little eye on *you*.'

# Chapter Five

Against strong headwinds it took another two whole days to reach Callalabasa, two tense days for Kit, at every moment sensing Mr Skinner's cold blue eyes upon him watching his every movement; and as luxurious as the royal airbarge was it suddenly seemed very cramped, so Kit was for ever being thrown into the detective's company. Even when Mr Skinner wasn't around, Kit imagined him there—a shadowy presence in a corner—and he got into the routine of peering around doors and checking over his shoulder.

On top of that he had to get used to life without magic. That wasn't easy. Constantly he had to remind himself to get up to fetch something rather than his lazy wizard way of pointing and have it fly itself over; while all the while the warm flame of magic flickered deep inside him, tempting and teasing.

No wonder he was so irritable and jumpy. Henry put it down to a case of plain old-fashioned moodiness.

'You wouldn't have a clue 'bout it, Henry,' Kit told him. 'You're not a wizard so I wouldn't 'spect you to understand; but when you're full up with magic it's the most natural thing in the world to use it—if you don't it feels like it will burst out of you anyway.'

Henry smiled sympathetically, yet Kit could tell it was all way beyond him.

Being so brim-full of magic was not without consequences: it probably made Kit more rash than usual, more willing to take a risk—perhaps he might have done what he did in any case; but very early on the second morning he slid out of bed and crept barefoot to the hold. If he was found out by Mr Skinner or anyone else, his excuse was ready prepared—he was worried about Carpet, couldn't sleep because of it, and was checking to see it was all right . . .

Not meeting a soul, however, he slipped through the hold door, the bare metal floor striking cold upon his feet. Without a pause or second thought as to the promise he had made to Henry, he pointed at the leather wireless box. A satisfying stream of magic flowed from him and he heard the delicious pop of exploding valves.

Kit smiled. 'There, Mr Skinner, try calling your friends now.' And feeling much better he made his way back to his cabin.

Then they arrived at their destination, the little country on the edge of every map.

Having never before heard of Callalabasa, Kit didn't have a clue what to expect. He peered with interest through a porthole. Instead of a docking-tower or a proper balloondrome he saw a ruined castle in a dusty field, the tallest tower converted to a mooring point. Already two airbarges were tied up there, a red one with a menacing dark eagle on its side, from Hohenzollernia; a black and yellow checked one topped with a golden crown, from Borrgunburg.

Nesting storks flew up as the *Flying George* inched its way closer, nose first, to join them. Ropes were tossed to men who had appeared high up on a ledge. There was a soft bump. China rattled and an apple rolled from the fruit bowl; and several sizeable blocks of stone fell from the tower. A group of people waiting below scattered yelling just before the blocks thudded on the ground, each block leaving a deep impression.

After that the engines died, the propellers slowed to a

halt, and the storks glided back down to their untidy nests.

Led by Henry smiling his charming smile, the passengers disembarked to be met by a swarm of plump generals in ridiculously elaborate uniforms and plumed hats. They flashed broad white smiles all around. 'So pleased, so pleased,' they chorused, smiling even broader and nodding their feathered heads like ducks. 'Good you come, hello, good day, howdy, top of the morning to you.'

Slinking up behind, Mr Skinner appeared at Kit's elbow like an unsummoned genie.

'Remember—*no magic*,' he whispered harshly. 'Not unless you intend to make big trouble for yourself.'

'I know—I know,' said Kit sullenly. He had just said his goodbyes to Carpet and was feeling in low spirits because Carpet, not understanding the reason it was being left behind, had struggled to come with him. In the end there was nothing for it but to turn on his heels and walk away. Defiantly he dug his hand deep into his pocket and flicked a spark from finger to finger.

'Ahhh, the young prince!'

A short, smiling man in a tasselled fez suddenly loomed up in front of him, holding out his hand, obviously mistaking him for Henry.

Not thinking properly, Kit pulled out his hand and the spark dropped to the floor and disappeared between the floorboards like a sparkling diamond. The man in the fez didn't appear to notice; Mr Skinner gave a withering glare.

Mumbling and awkward, Kit looked away; but then Henry, who was more practised at this sort of thing, stepped forward and with a few light words stopped this instance of mistaken identity from becoming a horrible embarrassment.

'Stay beside me where I can see you,' Mr Skinner hissed into Kit's ear. 'You aren't to be trusted on your own.'

At the foot of the tower a brass oompah band played the Callalabasian national anthem and the breeze gusted strongly across the dusty field, ruffling the double-headed bears that appeared on most of the flags, with a few Union Jacks scattered politely here and there. The generals pointed and laughed at each other, forced to clutch their plumed hats to their heads. Kit thought them remarkably playful for generals, they reminded him more of fat jolly butchers and landlords—red faced from too much of their own sausage and beer.

Drawn up in front of the band stood a line of horses and carriages; Kit stared at them. There was so much gold and the horses' coats were groomed to shining. Henry, who had a good eye and fondness for horses, was just as impressed and made a complimentary remark.

'Tell me, what kind of horses are they?' he asked.

The little man in the fez sighed. 'Pure-bred Austrian Lippizaners,' he said. 'The finest of the fine. But still only horse flesh when all is said and done.' He shrugged. 'It makes me so sad: if only Callalabasa were as rich and forward-looking as your country, Prince, then we could enjoy the wonders of steam-driven machines and our children would learn about horses and carriages in history books. I tell you they'd laugh themselves silly that the world was ever the way it was.'

'Duke,' said Henry steering him over, 'I would like you to meet my very good friend Kit Stixby. Kit, this is Duke Liechenspit, uncle of Eugen the new king.'

The duke bowed graciously; Kit bowed back less so, his bow suggesting he was doing his best to avoid a low door. He scowled to see Henry grinning at him, and had he been any nearer he would have kicked Henry on the shin, prince or no prince. As for Duke Liechenspit, he appeared a mild man, but his dark eyes moved quickly and his ever-present smile gave away nothing of what he thought.

He led the way across to the carriages. He, Henry, Kit, and Mr Skinner climbed aboard the first; the generals, giggling like naughty schoolboys, clambered into the others, one general poking another's bottom as he squeezed it through a narrow doorway. This was seen as hugely funny by the rest and they laughed until their medals jangled.

When the carriages were full (the ones loaded with generals sitting low on their axles) a whip cracked and they set off down the unpaved track, rocking on potholes and throwing up clouds of powdery yellow dust behind.

Thankfully the journey was a short one, for Kit quickly grew bored with the duke wittering on about their flight and the weather and the health of Henry's grandmother: it showed in his restless fidgeting and huffed out breath, so that Mr Skinner was forever nudging him to sit still. It was almost a relief when Luca, the capital city, came into view; Kit turned to gaze out of the window at it.

'Why, there's a mountain right in the middle,' he said with a giggle of disbelief. 'And look at all them steeples and domes high up on the top. That must be the king's palace, I suppose.'

The duke nodded. 'Not at all like your noble Buckingham Palace,' he murmured apologetically. 'See, on that side of the mountain the royal palace, on the other, the cathedral—St Basil-still-standing—such a second-rate building when I think of the splendours of Westminster Abbey . . . '

Kit studied the buildings carefully, but it was impossible to tell where the palace ended and the cathedral began; or for that matter where the soaring rock became either, blending towers and pinnacles so seamlessly. As a general rule, however, walls were pink, domes gold, and spires and window-shutters candy-striped; lesser roofs were covered in glazed peacock-blue tiles that sparkled at the edges where they caught the sunlight. Larger roofs were even more colourful—and elaborately patterned, the tiles on the largest roof of all having been arranged into the shape of a double-headed bear. If this were not impressive enough, facing them on their approach was a fabulous astrological clock ablaze with gold, scarlet, and silver; although the duke sniffingly admitted to a greater affection for Big Ben—it kept better time.

Altogether—crag, palace, cathedral—created the kind of mad jumble that made Kit want to cheer just to see it, it was so ridiculously improbable—like a lord dancing with a poodle.

Then, rattling under a gateway, the line of carriages entered Luca, Kit by now half hanging out of the carriage window determined not to miss a thing. He saw crumbling old buildings and donkeys drinking at fountains; women with baskets and chickens that flew up squawking between the horses' hooves. There were shops with brightly coloured awnings, carts of strange vegetables, men drinking coffee, clamouring beggars, and brass pots hung up for sale. . .

Nor was this an end to the many sights, but just then Mr Skinner tugged at Kit's jacket and he fell back into his seat with a thud. Kit glared at him briefly before returning his attention to a lively market place outside.

'So unlike your charming Regent Street with all its pretty gas-lit shops,' observed the duke.

Henry, who was gazing through the other window just as keenly as Kit, suddenly turned to him.

'Why does every door in Luca have an eye painted

above it, Duke? Is it some quaint custom. I must admit it gives me the oddest feeling, as if the buildings are spying on me.'

Duke Liechenspit shifted uncomfortably. 'The people are very simple here, Prince. They believe certain things. They think the eyes will ward off evil—the evil that comes from magic.'

Kit immediately prickled. 'But surely not *all* magic is evil,' he said, ignoring Mr Skinner's warning look. 'Well, in England it isn't; in England even Queen Victoria has her own witch doctor.' And smiling sweetly at the detective he added, 'And an amazin' doctor he is too—or so I'm told—his magic the best there is. Don't you have no witch doctors like him out here in Callalabasa?'

The duke's eyes were dark and faintly disturbing. 'Understand, Mr Stixby, in Callalabasa enchanters are not the same as your English ones; they are wild savages who thrive on the dark arts, they take what they want and curse those who get in their way. They are dogs, Mr Stixby, and deserve to be driven away like dogs.' His eyes softened. 'Your fine English wizards and witches are charming I'm sure—*in England*.'

Mr Skinner cleared his throat, and changing the subject said, 'I believe we have arrived at the palace, Duke.'

The line of carriages drew to a halt.


Because King Eugen's many-towered palace sat high up on sheer rock the only way to reach it was by a wicker basket winched up by a gang of palace servants. This took time: the company had to wait for the basket to be lowered—then the baggage arrived and servants came swarming out bringing refreshments for everyone. *'Yaho!'* shouted the jolly generals sinking more beer than anyone else.

Henry stood in polite conversation with the duke, discussing nothing in particular. He was good at that. Kit wasn't—a grunt did for him when he had nothing better to say; so he found himself alone with the bustle of their arrival going on all around.

Stepping back to be out of the way, he caught sight of Mr Skinner and took an immediate interest.

Thinking himself unobserved, the detective had sidled over to a servant girl and was talking earnestly to her. The girl held a tray of empty beer mugs, her eyes downcast and she was nodding. Her skin was tanned and she had almond-shaped eyes and very long dark shiny hair. Sly looking, thought Kit. And she just kept nodding her head as Mr Skinner talked at length to her.

'What on earth can he be saying?' wondered Kit. It was most odd. The oddest part was how they managed to understand each other at all: a simple palace girl was unlikely to know English and an untravelled detective would hardly be fluent in . . . well, whatever they spoke here in Callalabasa. Unless . . . *unless* this was an agreed meeting in the first place and both were more than they appeared.

'Of course!' said Kit, deciding at once what he must do. Pretending to be overcome with a sudden bout of tiredness, he sank down, closed his eyes and sent his mind out walking.

As an experienced mind-walker he knew he could not enter Mr Skinner's head or the head of the serving-girl without them realizing, but this did not mean all was lost. Around their feet, pecking at the dust, strutted a few stray pigeons—perfect for Kit if they were in earshot.

He sent his mind swiftly across to the nearest bird and it slipped effortlessly into its honeycombed skull, marvelling at the tininess of the brain it found inside—a brain which also tickled, because birds' brains are covered all over in fine feathers. Like a cushion turned inside out. Not that anyone actually ever sees them, yet most people are well aware of what stupid feather-brained creatures birds really are.

This particular one was no more intelligent than any other of its kind. As it pecked for grit it counted to itself—and like birds everywhere it knew only how to count up to three.

*One, two, three, more than three, more than three, more than three* . . .

Mr Skinner's voice could be heard in the distance but only as a senseless mumble.

*Go closer to the wall*, whispered Kit, and the pigeon, believing this one of its own thoughts making a suggestion, trooped happily across to where Kit wanted it.

Mr Skinner's voice sharpened into words.

' . . . I tell you, Tita, we must keep close tabs on his movements at all times, he could upset everything, he has the makings of a complete disaster.'

Kit guessed who he meant and felt strangely flattered.

Then he heard the girl speak.

'I'll do what I can to help, Mr Skinner, but I don't want to make anyone suspicious. I'm only supposed to be a servant and servants go where they are told.'

'I know that, but there is one thing you can definitely do. At the first possible opportunity go through his bag, find anything connected with magic and—'

Kit heard no more. A sinister spiky shadow flickered over the pigeon and it let out a squawk of terror.

*Cat!*

Then it took to the air, wings clattering; Kit's mind rolled to the back of its skull then tumbled out altogether. It fell through the air spinning and out of control.

*Ouch!*

Hitting the ground it bounced several times and rolled along in the dust before Kit finally managed to bring it to a halt. Thoughts, ideas, and memories were churned up together as it flew crookedly back to his body. Kit opened his eyes and saw double. When he tried to stand he was surprised how dizzy he was, staggering to keep upright.

'Kit!' said Henry a little shocked.

Mr Skinner pulled his mouth thin and disapproving.

The jolly generals hooted. One held up a tankard of foaming beer. 'Too strong for the English boy, eh? Ha-ha-ha.'


Kit was fully recovered by the time he was winched up in the basket, Henry, Duke Liechenspit, and Mr Skinner his fellow passengers; Mr Skinner as unfriendly as ever.

'I tell you it was the heat,' Kit had protested feebly; he knew the detective suspected more, he suspected magic!

They were lifted to the palace in a series of little jerks, the servants hauling them up in measured lengths of the rope, singing to keep rhythm. The basket swayed and creaked at every pull; and Kit might have been more concerned about it had he not been fully occupied surveying the ground below.

Henry watched, amused. 'What exactly are you so interested in?' he asked.

'Oh nothin' . . . Is that our luggage they're unloading down there?'

Kit pointed.

'I suppose . . .'

'What will happen to it?'

'I expect Dummock and the palace servants will see to it in a minute,' said Henry. 'Isn't that so, Duke?'

'Oh indeed. The servants are very good and trustworthy

in Callalabasa . . . Maybe not quite so top notch as your English ones. Ah, the last time I stayed at Claridges . . . '

Eventually, on reaching the palace, they were helped out onto a paved platform, Kit still glancing down and fretful about his bag and what might become of it if that girl—Tita—got to it first.

'This way, gentlemen,' said Duke Liechenspit holding out his hand in an elegant gesture. 'I know his majesty, King Eugen, is looking forward to meeting you.'

The breeze blew fresh and cool through the palace, blowing no doubt from the distant mountain range they saw shimmering beneath the morning sun. Curtains billowed out over doorways. Strolling and chatting amiably, the duke led them into a tiled hall with a wooden ceiling and stags' antlers over every window and door. Kit immediately threw up his hands to cover his ears. About five hundred very large and beautifully carved cuckoo clocks were tick-tocking away on the wall, pendulums swaying in time with each other.

'An unfortunate custom,' explained the duke almost shouting. 'At every possible royal occasion—birthdays, coronations, deaths—the Guild of Cuckoo Clock Makers insists on presenting the palace with a gift. And as you might well imagine, their gift without fail has been—'

'A cuckoo clock!' laughed Henry.

'Precisely.' The duke shuddered. 'So quaint and utterly old-fashioned . . . I'd advise you to hurry, Prince. It's nearly up to the hour and this is not the place to linger when all the cuckoos go off together. Legend has it that several maids have been driven mad.'

Kit grinned. 'You might well say they went cuckoo.'

Mr Skinner's stony look made him regret he had ever spoken.

Quickly leaving the hall of cuckoo clocks behind they went up some marble stairs, under an arch supported by two stone ogres, and through a set of doors into a long narrow room.

The room was very grand but also rather solemn and gloomy because its windows were few and small, and its chandeliers unlit; it was further darkened by a vast painting that covered every inch of wall and ceiling space: King Buba the Half Beard and his army defeating the Magyar Vampires. There were buckets of blood and heaps of garlic and people getting chopped up (or bitten) all over the place. Not the best of rooms to enjoy a peaceful Sunday morning breakfast, observed Kit. Suits of armour lined the walls like clockwork soldiers, their helmets eye-catchingly made in the likeness of real or imagined animals; and double-headed bear flags hung over them.

At the far end on a simple wooden throne sat the King—Eugen XIV—or at least they believed him to be the king, for his face was hidden behind a book and he trembled visibly. Approaching a little nearer, it could be seen that the book was upside down.

Everyone bowed, except Kit, who was too engrossed in a scene of a Magyar vampire being run through by a vicious barbed sword, until Mr Skinner's hand found the grubby back of his neck and bent it for him.

Then Duke Liechenspit glided forward to stand beside the throne; he cleared his throat, bent down and began to whisper in the king's ear, but so echoey was the hall that it was impossible not to overhear his every word.

'Majesty, your guests from England have arrived.'

Still hidden by the book, the king whispered back in his own language.

'English—English, your majesty,' interrupted the duke. 'Remember your lessons. Our guests will not understand you.'

'I d-don't think I want them to,' said the king. 'What

am I to do, uncle? I d-don't know what to say to them—and they're expecting me to say something, aren't they? Perhaps something witty or clever. And what if I try to say something witty and they don't laugh? Oh, I'm hopeless at this sort of thing—absolutely hopeless. Can't you send them away, uncle, or tell them that I've lost my voice? My throat does feel a little sore now I come to think about it. I know, *you* say something.'

He gripped the book so tightly and sounded so desperate that Duke Liechenspit must have taken pity on him; he straightened, took a breath, and staring straight over everyone's head spoke out in the booming voice of authority.

'His most wise and noble majesty, King Eugen, commands me to speak on his behalf and bid his illustrious guests from England a heartfelt welcome. He says this day shall be numbered among the greatest days in the history of his country and it pleases him beyond a sultan's riches that you have set foot in his fair kingdom; he sincerely looks forward to warm and friendly relations with you, your government, and your people from this day forth and for ever more.'

'I-I do?'

King Eugen was unexpectedly peering over his book—an awkward-looking youth of about eighteen.

'You do,' said the duke firmly.

'Well then,' said the king, putting aside the book completely and sounding much relieved. 'That's got that out of the way. Didn't go so badly did it?'


Shortly after, Henry and Kit were shown to their rooms. A servant in a handsome green uniform and powdered wig led Henry away to his; Kit went in the opposite direction, forced to follow a stooped old fellow who smelt of fish and whose hacking cough was not quite as awful as his habit of spitting on the stairs.

By this, Kit knew that someone at the palace had mistaken him for Henry's servant. Probably they had examined the guest list and not finding his name upon it had assumed the rest themselves. It was an easy mistake to make, quite understandable. Even in Henry's borrowed clothes no one would mistake Kit for a prince—but a *servant*. Naturally Henry would think it highly amusing when he found out about it later, laughing his head off and making great play of it by ordering him around.

'Huh, just let him try,' growled Kit to himself.

The old man plodded on: he didn't speak or pretend to be interested in Kit in any way, but led him deeper and deeper into the palace where it was a little less grand, a little more shabby—pink paint peeling off the walls and patches of damp on the ceiling.

Suddenly Kit stopped dead in his tracks and the old man turned and stared at him sourly, wondering what was wrong.

'Oh . . . sorry, it's nothing important,' murmured Kit, continuing to follow him. But it was.

He had seen Tita. Almost before he had recognized her she had swept past looking pale and grim.

'In—in!' motioned the old man abruptly, opening the same door through which Tita had appeared only seconds before, *the door to his room.*

Kit hesitated a moment then stepped in alone. The room was small and not particularly clean. Pipes from other rooms crossed the ceiling and the mirror was flaked and cracked.

Yet Kit's eyes fell on none of these things. He was staring straight ahead at the bed.

On it his bag had been emptied out. In a tangled heap lay the remains of his wizard robes; his wand broken into a dozen pieces. And more . . . Slowly Kit reached out and touched a fragment of wand then gazed in horror at his finger tips.

*Fresh blood.*

Feeling sick he frantically wiped his hand on his trousers then hurriedly hid the remains of his belongings under the mattress before anyone had the chance to come in and see them. He was angry and frightened. But there was no doubt in his mind as to the meaning behind this. It was a warning—a warning from Mr Skinner and his fellow magic-haters. It was their way of telling him to be careful of what he got mixed up in, because if he didn't he'd best watch out . . . they were not afraid to spill blood.

# Chapter Six

Although much had happened in a short space of time, the day was still barely into the early part of the afternoon and the sun rode high in the sky. Kit set out to find Henry, the servants happy to point him in the right direction if he stopped them and asked, 'English prince?' in a loud enough voice. Already Kit had resolved not to tell his friend anything about the frenzied attack on his possessions and the warning in blood; he had no firm evidence to lay the blame at Mr Skinner's door and until he had, he would say nothing.

When he finally reached it, he discovered Henry's room far more lavish than he'd expected. It had a wide balcony lined with orange trees, its own fountain, and furniture the like of which Kit had only before seen in museums, and then usually accompanied by a 'Do not touch' sign. The bed alone was the size of Kit's room, with a complete tree trunk at each corner for a bed-post, and climbing the trunks were brass bears—double-headed ones at that—standing as tall as fully grown mountain bears and each wearing a heavy spiked and jewelled collar. Not the sort of thing Kit cared to wake up to in the middle of a dark night, but impressive nevertheless.

Half lost amidst so much splendour was a rather impatient looking Henry. He had changed into a military outfit and was standing on a stool, while Dummock fussed around him, pins in mouth, trying to secure loose hems.

'Dummock thinks I've grown since we left London,'

said Henry by way of a greeting, seeing Kit slip round the door.

'Oh.'

Henry glanced at him, frowning. 'What's wrong with you? Bellyache from too much magic? You seem to be in as foul a mood as Mr Skinner.'

Kit looked up, suddenly interested.

'Last time I saw him,' continued Henry having an arm lifted by Dummock, 'he was storming off somewhere muttering something about finding a new set of valves.'

Kit smiled slyly.

'I don't suppose you would happen to know anything about that, would you, Kit?' Henry raised a suspicious eyebrow at him.

'*Me?*' cried Kit pretending to be shocked. 'Why should I know summat about some stupid valves? That's the trouble with science, it keeps breaking down, nothin' ever lasts.'

Henry rubbed an itch on the end of his nose. 'Prince— Prince, please try to keep still,' squawked Dummock exasperated.

To annoy him further, Henry rubbed his nose for a whole minute longer than was necessary.

'Anyway, why you all done up like a toy soldier?' asked Kit, tilting his head and studying him, as if just noticing for the first time the braiding, epaulettes, and sharp military cut of his jacket.

'Dress rehearsal this afternoon.'

'For what?'

'The coronation, you idiot. Why do you think I'm here in the first place?'

Kit shrugged. 'Never realized a coronation needed to be rehearsed.'

'Well it does, and it's dreary, and I feel like a tailor's dummy. And look—' Ignoring Dummock's tuts he drew out his sword. 'The blade's wooden,' he said darkly. 'Grandmama insisted. She said there was no chance I would cut myself on a wooden sword. The shame of it. What if someone challenges me to a duel, what am I supposed to do with *this*?'

'Could try giving him a nasty splinter,' suggested Kit smiling. 'You never know, it might eventually go septic.'

With a huge sigh of relief Dummock stuck in the final pin; he helped Henry out of his jacket, and Henry jumped free of the stool.

'How about you, Kit, how will you spend the rest of the afternoon?'

Kit shrugged. 'Dunno, hang about the palace, I suppose.' But to himself he had already decided to try to get back down into the city and do a little exploring. It was far easier now Mr Skinner was not around.


The palace was exceedingly busy: princes, duchesses, and prime ministers strolled along balconied terraces towards the cathedral, making as common a sight as sparrows in the park; top hats and diamond tiaras two a penny.

Using the cover of so many people, Kit headed towards the wicker basket lift, sure that no one followed. He walked with a swagger in his step, pleased at his own cleverness. But this quickly turned to dismay when he reached the lift. The hard-muscled winch-winders who operated it stood around talking amongst themselves.

'Excuse me—excuse me,' said Kit politely.

One of the men turned and eyed him suspiciously; he spat through his front teeth then turned back.

He doesn't recognize me, thought Kit. He thinks I'm nobody important otherwise I'd be at the cathedral for the rehearsal. Then he remembered that while making his way to Henry's room he had seen a second lift which, like the back stairs in a big house, was meant for servants. He hurried to find it again. To his immense relief the winchmen there proved much more obliging.

'Me—down, please,' he said pointing groundwards. The men nodded, standing aside to let him clamber into the basket. Creakily it started to descend.

Now, being the servants' lift it was situated on a less pleasant side of the palace, the side that was workaday and not especially pleasing on the eye. Going down, Kit first passed storerooms, their windows white with cobwebs; then he came upon the kitchens, steam billowing out of vents, and pipes emptying directly from the walls, coating the rock with hardened dribbles of fat like dirty candle runs. Dishwashers stared blankly at him and the clatter of pans was unending.

At the next level the windows were no bigger than holes cut into the mountainside and meanly barred; and the instant Kit guessed this to be the dungeon, the basket stopped dead and he was left hanging in mid air.

The basket swung from side to side. The ropes creaked. Shading his eyes Kit glanced up but could see nothing of the winch or the men who operated it.

'Wonder what the matter is?' he muttered.

He asked the question to himself, yet a strange croaky voice spoke out in reply.

'Ah, the machinery is very old, sir, old and too often used. It is not uncommon for the rope to slip and the spool to jam. Do not alarm yourself unduly, sir, all will be made well in a minute or two.'

Kit turned around but saw no one. 'Who's there?' he whispered.

Slowly a face appeared at a barred window on the same level as the basket, a face so white and bloodless that Kit shivered. And despite being all of the man there was to see, Kit sensed a great deal more—something cold and stonelike at his centre.

But this was silly, Kit had only just met him; he studied the stranger closely. He saw that his head was completely hairless and his bloodshot eyes strained against the sun; his ears were so tiny that they resembled fleshy unfurled flowers and his lips were coloured an unnatural red. He was old, without question, but so alert and watchful it was impossible to guess his age; and although full of intelligence, Kit had to admit it was not the kind of face anyone might easily warm to.

'Do not be alarmed by me or your situation,' continued the man quietly. 'The basket often gets jammed outside my window; it is how I receive my only visitors these days . . . My name is Count Drohlomski. I am pleased to meet you, my little English friend.'

He bowed briefly and Kit heard the click of heels.

'Are you . . . are you a prisoner for something you did wrong?' whispered Kit, slightly more inquisitive than repulsed by the sinister little man.

Count Drohlomski lifted his hands to the bars; his long gnarled nails made Kit gasp.

'Oh, young sir, my crimes are not fit for such tender young ears as yours. Terrible—terrible. It is enough to say that when I was put into this tiny cell they threw away the key, and when I die my bones will be burned and their ashes scattered in many places.'

'But that's horrible,' cried Kit. 'Nobody deserves to be treated so badly, whatever they've done.'

Count Drohlomski smiled then stopped; he stared at Kit, a hard unfathomable gleam in his eyes. 'Come, step closer,' he urged. 'Step to the edge of the basket; I'm sure you wouldn't say no to shaking hands with an old man who hasn't a single friend in the world. You would not refuse to grant such a simple request.'

70

Kit didn't move; he wondered what it would be like to touch those long horny talons that were more animal than human.

'Well . . . I s'pose. It can't do any real harm now, can it?' he said.

The count narrowed his eyes contentedly and reached out his hand further, a scrap of filthy lace trailing from his cuff.

Kit stretched out his own hand to meet it, he could feel the basket tipping slightly . . . Nearly there—

Suddenly all manner of angry shouts broke out above and the winch-winders began hurling stones—not at Kit as far as he could make out, but at the count. Stones bounced and rattled down the walls.

'Stop it!' shouted Kit horrified, but then the lift became unstuck and he fell back as the basket went hurtling towards the ground. It struck it hard and Kit spilled out.

Unhurt but angry he jumped up. Searching the palace's lower parts he saw only endless barred windows; of Count Drohlomski's cell there was no longer a trace.

Kit kicked a stone and, feeling out of sorts with the world, marched away from the palace's chilly shadow and went into the streets of Luca. It was a while before he had calmed down enough to explore it properly.

He soon found Luca was not like other cities he knew—not like Paris and certainly not like London. For a start the streets were free of heavy traffic and what little there was, was donkey-powered not steam. The same was true of the sky. Not a single balloon bicycle (let alone a decent sized airship) was to be seen anywhere amongst all that endless blue, and a pair of buzzards who circled effortlessly above made Kit realize that such a sight would be considered near miraculous back home in London.

The absence of traffic and power-lines was noticeable, unfortunately so too was the number of beggars who

71

pestered him for pennies; while the poorer quarters of Luca struck him as much grimmer than the slum parts of the East End of London he knew. Yet however tumbled down a hovel was, however grassy the thatch or crumbling the walls, there was always one thing that was freshly painted and cared for—the eye above the doorway.

'The people here must really be afraid of magic,' said Kit sadly.

Then, turning a corner, he unexpectedly came across an unpleasant scene in a back street.

A band of uniformed men (Kit guessed they were some kind of policemen) had stopped a poor country farmer and were rummaging through the fruit and vegetables on his cart. The police were snarling at each other and at the old farmer who pleaded with them to be more careful, as already three melons lay smashed upon the cobbles. Despite their search, the police had not found what they were looking for, and this much was reported to their superior officer, who leant uncaringly against a wall: a fat, unshaven individual in a uniform so tight that the buttons pulled and his belly swelled over his belt.

The old man, hands together and head bowed, dared to approach and beg him to be allowed to continue on his way. The fat police captain regarded him coldly a moment, then his gloved hand flashed out and tore open the old man's shirt.

In that briefest of moments, before the old man covered up his chest again, Kit glimpsed a tiny charm around his neck—a safeguard against rheumatism, most like—yet it was magic and enough to seal the old man's fate. He was speedily arrested. Wailing pitifully he was taken away to police headquarters, his donkey cart led after him, already the grinning policemen helping themselves to fruit.

Kit felt sick. In his mouth was a bitter taste and his stomach churned. This, he realized, was magic. It swept from his stomach, down through his arms into his hands. His fingers tingled. It was not in his nature to stand by and do nothing at all; and, as far as he was concerned, if Mr Skinner had any objections he could go boil his head!

Daring to take the risk, he pointed—although not in an obvious way, he was not so stupid as to try to draw attention to himself with a grand and noble gesture. His hand moved ever so slightly and he felt a steady stream of magic flow from him. A second later the back of the cart crashed down and brightly coloured fruit cascaded out.

As hoped, the sight of so much free food proved too much for the street beggars. Driven by hunger they dived forward, dodging kicks and blows from the police.

Kit pointed again. This time the nearest two policemen began scratching themselves all over. They itched madly, as did the others by now, rubbing their backs up and down against a wall and howling curses. None suspected magic. By the way they shunned the beggars it was clear they imagined themselves infested by great biting fleas. The beggars didn't care what they thought so long as they were free to enjoy their banquet; and the old man, coming to his senses, seized his chance and slipped quietly away.

Kit watched him go.

'Best I make myself scarce too,' he muttered. 'That itching curse won't last much longer and I'd hate to be around when it ends.'

He turned and walked quickly down a narrow alley and almost immediately sensed he was being followed. He stopped and his follower stopped with him. He set off again walking more briskly; behind him the pace was matched step for step.

A wave of apprehension passed over Kit, shrinking his magic to a small purple-blue flame. He broke into a run then stopped abruptly. Someone had called after him and the voice was that of a woman.

Slowly Kit turned to see.

The woman was poor, so poor she had no shoes and the edges of her clothes were ragged; her face was pale with worry. Bundled in her arms she cradled something precious to her, and as she crept closer she spoke pleadingly to Kit in her own language.

Kit lowered his eyes to see inside the bundle was a small child. With his wizard's sight he saw the purple cloud of fever hovering about the youngster's head, coming as a vapour from his nose and mouth, and gusting around him whenever he coughed.

The woman must have seen Kit perform his magic, and now she begged him to use that same power on her sick infant.

Kit found what she asked was daunting.

'I'll try my best,' he said hesitantly. 'But believe me I'm not half so good at this kind of thing as my dad.'

The woman nodded, trying to understand, her big dark eyes watching his every movement.

'Well, if you're sure you trust me,' said Kit, trying desperately to remember what his father would do to dispel a fever. 'Ah, yes . . . what about this—'

He began, moving his hands over the child's head. He knew what he did was dangerous, not least because someone might pass by at any moment and a complete fool could tell he was weaving a spell. But Kit also had a bigger worry. He wasn't a properly trained witch doctor— what if he used too much magic and over-cured the child, ending up doing more harm than good? Pushing the thought aside, he spoke the clearing charm, hoping it would take effect quickly.

And it did. Vapour started to leak thickly from the child, more black now than purple and smelling horrible as it was expelled. Unlike before it did not hover around the child waiting to be breathed back in, but swirled up into the air and vanished. Soon the vapour was thin and running out; a minute later it was gone.

Kit smiled and the woman smiled too, sobbing out a joyful laugh when the child opened his eyes at her.

'Mama?' he said sleepily.

'Bahbu,' laughed the woman hugging him tightly.

The happy moment was brief, ended by a furious shout from the top of the alley. Startled, Kit looked past the woman and her child to see the fat police captain in the tight uniform, glaring at him; his trousers splattered in peaches and other pulpy fruit. With clumsy, podgy fingers he fumbled in his shirt pocket, took out a whistle and blew it until his eyes bulged.

In a flash the woman grabbed Kit's hand and they were off, running through alleys so narrow and twisting that not once did a beam of sunlight flicker upon them.

Behind, the shrill whistling pursued them, coming in breathless bursts and each time the woman gripped Kit's hand more tightly. They dodged left and right. Despite bare feet the woman was surprisingly swift and Kit wondered where she was taking him.

Suddenly she pushed him through a low doorway into a thatched hovel consisting of a single, clean room with two hard chairs and a rickety table; a cooking fire at one end and a bed of straw covered in blankets at the other. The floor was bare earth. As the door flew open a large friendly dog bounded up from the fireside. The woman spoke to it harshly and pointed out into the alley; the dog dashed out, growling, and the woman closed the door behind it, putting up a finger to her lips at Kit to be silent.

Soon a small group of policemen were outside. They sounded edgy. They had not expected the dog which came as a nasty surprise, for far from being friendly any more it bared its teeth and snapped at them. Kit watched from a tiny window as the dog lunged at the fat captain's ankles, forcing him into a kind of galumphing dance, sweat glistening on his face and moustache.

Kit laughed. 'Far less high and mighty now,' he said.

# Chapter Seven

With two hours left before sundown, Kit remained with Bahbu and his mother, really having no choice; for every time he tried to edge towards the door in an attempt to leave, the woman leapt up and blocked his way, shooing him back into the room—making it very plain it was not yet safe to go.

So Kit made himself useful in a wizardly kind of way. He cured a wart on the woman's thumb and hung a charm in the chimney to make it draw better. Immediately the dense acrid smoke started to clear and Kit's eyes stopped smarting. For the dog, which had returned home everyone's hero, Kit had a special reward, ridding its coat of all the troublesome bugs and mites. The dog stopped mid scratch and stared at Kit, ears cocked in astonishment.

The woman was content to busy herself in her own way. Singing softly she swung an iron pot over the fire and began the evening meal, soon filling the room with the smell of good wholesome food. Bahbu played with Kit who was happy to amuse him with bubbles and fireflies; easy magic as far as Kit was concerned, but then he turned and eyed the woman thoughtfully. Her back was to him, bent over the pot as she stirred her stew, pausing to taste it and add more pepper. The last thing Kit wanted was to alarm her or frighten her in any way—but he felt it was worth a try.

His mind went out to her and to his surprise she let him in at once, her thoughts speaking to him in a way her tongue could not.

*My name is Voma Taslavia,* she said. *And I thank you with all my heart for what you have done for Bahbu, my own dear boy.*

*But I am a wizard,* said Kit. *Why aren't you afraid of me like all the others?*

She paused. *I come from the mountains where you magic people are still respected; it is only in the towns and cities that things are different and people are afraid. My husband, Niko, he comes from the mountains too. That is where he is now. He went to find a witch who will sell him a cure for Bahbu. We are not rich, as you can see, we had to sell our only cupboard and brass candlesticks to raise enough money. But a day or two after he left, Bahbu grew worse. I was so worried. Then I saw you, a wizard-boy, and I watched you do your magic. I knew I could not let you slip away without begging you to help.*

*You took a big risk.*

*Yes . . . You saw for yourself how people who deal with enchanters are dealt with in return.*

*Ah yes, who was that big bully who tried to arrest the old man?*

He felt Voma Taslavia's contempt swirling around him. *Captain Alecu Slobbahn of the Magic Watch.*

*What's that?* asked Kit.

*The secret police. Huh, that fat pig! He does and takes whatever he wants and all in the name of hunting down enchanters and their work. We are terrified of him. He's far worse than the*—she stopped suddenly and Kit felt her mind snap shut like a clam before she could say too much.

Kit said, *I really must go now, it's getting dark. My friend Henry'll wonder where I am.*

*You can't!* she cried. *Luca is a wild place at night, and you are a stranger here—besides, see, I've made you some supper. Stay, please stay. Stay until morning at least.*

*I can't. Nobody knows I'm here and Henry'll be worried. No*

78

*doubt Mr Skinner will be wondering too, though for different reasons . . . Sorry but I really do have to go.*

Once Kit's mind had returned to his body, Voma Taslavia rose up, lit a candle, and placed it in the window so light would fall outside in the alley. Then she came back, took Kit's hands and to his deep embarrassment kissed his fingers.

'No—no!' cried Kit blushing furiously.

Voma Taslavia smiled. She opened the door, holding Bahbu in her arms. Kit shivered, surprised to find how cold the night was. Cold and dark.

Voma Taslavia spoke her goodbyes to him, Kit not understanding a single word but feeling their warmth. He smiled, waved his hand, and strode off into the darkness.

He walked briskly at first, confident he could remember his way back to the palace without much bother at all. Quickly he discovered he was wrong. The alleys seemed to possess a secret magic of their own at night, somehow able to shuffle themselves around and rearrange themselves in a baffling new order that led only to dead ends or back to where they started. On top of this there were no street lamps to help him, not here in the poorer part of Luca anyway; while on either side the buildings stood shoulder to shoulder, thickening the darkness with their shadows.

Not once did he meet another soul—or if he did they managed to slip by without him noticing, frightened that he might be a thief—or worse. Hopelessly lost and unable to see beyond the walls and roofs which tightly hemmed him in, he lost all sense of direction. If only he could have a single glimpse of the palace, it wasn't as if he didn't look for it—

'Oh!'

*Eyes* were the only things he saw with any regularity,

those horrible painted eyes. They were impossible to avoid. He had just to turn a corner and another one was bound to be there, shining through the darkness, making him jump. They looked so different now. By day they appeared crude and mildly laughable, but at night they turned sinister and all-seeing; stretched wide as in a glare—or scream: hard tiny pupils, red veins, eyelashes like rows of barbs.

Kit disliked them intensely, and seriously considered pointing up a glow-ball if only for the sake of its company. A faint light: it would have to be faint, his dispirited magic lurked so low inside him it was hardly sufficient to light a match.

He turned into a cobbled square, the first time the narrow alleys had opened out, and before him flickered a pair of feeble gas lamps. In the centre of the square, a fountain burbled eerily—a double-headed stone bear dribbling water, green slime upon its jaws and chest. Around it clustered crooked half-timbered shops, each with an elaborate metal sign showing the shopkeeper's business—a boot for the cobbler, a loaf of bread for the baker, a pig for the butcher.

Before he noticed much more, Kit was distracted by the urgent sound of running feet heading in his direction; and a few seconds later a gangly young man burst into the square, narrowly avoiding sprawling flat on his face. Kit stepped back into a doorway and watched; what struck him immediately was that the man had the same wide startled eyes as those painted above the doors. He ran around the square yelling at the top of his voice until the shopkeepers and their families showed themselves at upper windows, demanding to know what was going on.

'*Diya! Diya!*' cried the man pointing frantically in the direction from which he'd come.

Kit stepped further back into the shadows, wondering

what it might mean. The young man then raced away leaving behind an atmosphere thick with tension; agitated families shouting across the square to each other; and further off the jangle of harnesses and the sound of hooves clattering over cobbles. Kit stood perfectly still, sensing that whatever approached was responsible for stirring up these feelings of fear and panic. The horses were galloping nearer and nearer; and part of him wanted to tear himself away and run as fast as he could in the opposite direction.

But it was too late—into the square swept six horsemen riding six curse-black stallions, the creatures rolling their eyes and the veins standing out on their necks. Their flanks steamed, foam flecked their drawn-back lips, and their manes were wet and lank. They had been ridden hard and were nervous and difficult to control. One reared up, pedalling the air, whinnying nightmarishly.

Kit went cold all over.

Sitting upright in their saddles, he saw each rider was similarly dressed in a heavy robe (such as an old-fashioned wizard might wear); their hoods drawn up and not a single face visible. But from within the dark depths of the hoods, red eyes glowed steadily and devilishly like pinpricks of molten lava. All around, the shopkeepers and their families hurled insults at the riders and shook their fists, yet not a man stepped out to confront them. Some made the sign against evil, others dragged their families away and quietly bolted the shutters; fear and hatred could be smelt like the musty sweat of the horses.

Kit watched in growing disbelief. 'Surely nobody is taken in by this,' he told himself angrily. 'Nobody in their right mind can possibly believe them phoneys are proper enchanters.' And as he watched, one rider rode up to the fountain and cast in a handful of crystals. Immediately the water turned blood red.

Again Kit knew that the riders were behaving in a way many people who are fearful of magic expect enchanters to behave. They were poisoning the water, although it was as likely even this spiteful act was a pretence—a coloured dye as believable as the real thing.

Magic sparked at the corner of Kit's mouth. For a moment he was tempted to show these impostors what a genuine wizard could do. But then they wheeled around and galloped off, in parting shooting out flashes of white light from their sleeves.

Kit sniffed the air. 'Gunpowder,' he said deeply unimpressed; but he had seen enough to want to find out more and went chasing after, keeping watch from the shadows.

Like a band of well rehearsed actors, the riders went through their performance six or seven times more, choosing places where they were sure of a large audience. They seemed intent on scaring as many people as possible. Frequently their presence alone, sweeping in on their dark, half-wild horses, was more than sufficient to do that; other times they went through the play of poisoning wells and fountains, and shooting off fireworks like blasts of raw magic. Kit followed them from place to place, running to keep up, always just a few dozen paces behind—until they simply went and vanished.

Not slipped away from him but actually vanished off the face of the earth, as if by the very magic they so plainly lacked.

When it happened Kit hadn't been too far behind. He saw them rein their horses to the right and crowd into a narrow alleyway; there was no mistake about that. Yet on arriving at the same spot a few seconds later, he saw the alley was a dead end created by three solid walls without there being so much as a small window to offer any way out; and while the smell of horses remained as pungent on the air as ever, both they and their masters had mysteriously vanished.

Kit hovered, getting his breath back, wondering what to do next. Nothing for tonight, he decided, there was no time; so finding a stone he scratched a secret mark on the wall, one he would be able to recognize again. Then, reluctantly, he turned away and went towards the palace now clearly in view over the roof tops.

It was very late when he at last reached it, walking all the way round its rocky base only to arrive back where he started. Both baskets had been wound up and if there was a special way of summoning them—a bell, for instance—it was unknown to him.

'Bother!' he said, idly digging his heel into the mud. He felt hungry and tired, and did not relish the idea of staying on the streets of Luca a second longer than he had to. Voma Taslavia was right, they *were* wild.

Then, by a small inn across the way, he spotted a broomstick leaning against the wall and his heart leapt. It looked exactly the same as a flying broomstick; yet the moment he picked it up he felt only lifeless wood and twigs. Still, with a little bit of magical coaxing . . .

Standing back out of sight of the road and inn, Kit began to stroke the broomstick, working his magic into its grain until the handle gave a reluctant twitch and was still. It was a start, he supposed. Like all obedient things, flying brooms needed to be trained, but once they were they never forgot their training; this was the reason brooms were so regularly handed down in families, and why the best broomsticks were over a hundred years old. These nimble antiques had mastered how to turn and how to dive; how to slide down a breeze and how to hang still in a hurricane. They could navigate by the stars and remember complex routes, while the very best ones even allowed for the turning of the earth and changes in the wind. But first, long before training could commence, many different spells had to be woven about them, the more the better if a broom was to learn intricate manoeuvres. So, if ever you saw a witch flying across the sky in a careful straight line, chances were she was riding a brand-new broom, or it was Aunt Pearl out gathering toadstools.

But this is all by the by; Kit required a broom that would do one thing and one thing only—rise—the rest he could manage for himself thank you very much. And to his delight it started to do just that. He jumped on the handle, only to find himself the very next instant dumped in the dust; he blinked up at the broom as it hovered over him, looking dangerously ready to clout him around the ears. It had thrown him off like a bucking bronco. That's another thing worth remembering—new brooms are liable to be temperamental, they have to be broken in like a stubborn pony.

His dignity slightly dented, Kit wove several calming spells tightly through its twigs and tried again, this time with more success. Broom and wizard rose skywards together.

Oh, but it was so painfully slow—but worse than that the broom was clumsy, several times bumping into the palace's rocky side, grazing Kit's leg and ripping a gaping hole in his borrowed trousers (Dummock was not going to be pleased about that). With a swift hard kick of his foot, Kit pushed himself free. It became slightly better once unpredictable rock gave way to smooth pink wall. Kit made himself ready by crouching on the handle, waiting to launch himself clear at the very first opportunity that came his way.

Slowly up and up he went and to his dismay shuttered window followed shuttered window, with never a balcony or good clear terrace ever once appearing. Kit grew worried. He glanced up to see the palace's great astrological clock looming over him, its elaborate gilding glittering in the grey starlight. Across its face he noticed a platform and he remembered that at every quarter of the hour when the clock struck, a number of mechanical figures representing the symbols of the zodiac trooped out of a small door on the right, paraded along the platform and disappeared through a second door on the opposite side. Kit calculated this might be his only chance before the roofs, but it was not going to be easy; the platform was scarcely a few feet wide. In his chest his heart quickened, and his senses grew sharp; he wiped both sweaty palms on his bloodstained trousers.

The bottom of the clock was now only feet away . . . now inches . . . Kit was thankful that the lumpen broom was at least steady. His body felt tense; his muscles coiled as tight as a cat's before it pounces. He knew he had one chance. Just one. He licked his lips and—

He jumped, kicking his legs as he sprang—between the broom and the clock a sharp and sickening fall onto broken rocks below. His feet struck the platform; his shoulder collided with the clock face. Very nearly he bounced backwards but saved his life by grabbing the minute hand, yanking it down before finally steadying himself. Bells chimed, machinery whirled. Accidentally he had gone and tugged the time into the next quarter and a line of life-sized wooden figures rumbled out to meet him, the wheels they ran on made of solid iron and heavy enough to squash him flat.

Heading the twelve zodiac figures and acting as their champion was a knight in rusted armour, his face red and his nose as hooked as Mr Punch's at a seaside show; jerkily he swept a sword before him to clear the way, the point real if the sword was not.

Without room to step aside or time to catch his breath, Kit scrambled away on all fours, reached the second door and fell through it into dusty darkness, the measured clunk of heavy machinery sounding loudly in his ears. He dropped off the track. Seconds later the line of wooden figures crashed in after him then, abruptly, stopped dead. Kit waited a moment before pointing a glow-ball. When it came, it shook as much as his hand, taking a whole minute until the magic had set firm enough to cast a clear unblemished light.

By it he looked around at the strange new mechanical world he now found himself in. As a wizard he cared nothing about the workings of machines, yet the sheer size of the clock demanded that he paid it his fullest attention. Enclosed in a room as large as a house, the main driving-wheel towered up three times the height of a man; and connected to it or arranged around it, Kit saw gears and racks and ratchets; springs and levers and row upon row of bells. Little brass wheels whirled incessantly; the mighty one tocked and hardly moved at all, leaving Kit with the distinct impression it was not just recording time but actually creating it!

And as he stood amongst all this ancient machinery, Kit developed the curious feeling he was being watched—and not just watched but glared at. Stupid really, he told himself, but perhaps the feeling lingered from the city where those endless painted eyes had seemed to follow his every movement. And just as he was beginning to relax he saw them—two very furious, mercury-dark eyes in a distant corner, visible through a shock of fur, every single hair and whisker risen on end like steel needles. The instant it was spotted, the creature threw itself onto the Mr Punch knight and in a frenzy of incomprehensible rage tore at his chest with its brass claws then bit off the end of his nose.

Kit watched in alarm. The creature was very recognizably a gremlin—and if this was not surprising enough, it was Professor Muir's gremlin. It was Luddite!

'But how? That's impossible!'

Kit was still pondering on it when he stepped out of the clock through a small door at the back. He was so deep in thought he didn't pay attention to where he was going, yet the night had one last surprise in store for him—he walked straight into it unprepared.

'M-Mr Skinner!'

The detective stared at him from beneath the shadowy brim of his bowler hat. He was standing upon a high wall overlooking the city: in his hand a heavy signalling lamp smoked slightly from recent use, the filament inside glowing dimly as it cooled.

Kit recovered quickly and with a nod towards the lamp said cheerily, 'See you never got no more of them valves for that wireless set of yours, eh, Mr Skinner?'

In an unexpected fit of cold fury, Mr Skinner seized Kit's hand and glared at the blackened tips of his fingers. 'And I see you don't listen to warnings, boy. You've been using your magic again, haven't you? Playing with fire in more ways than one. You want to be careful you don't go and get yourself burned!'

Kit snatched back his hand and stared at him, then with a defiant crackle of magic he turned and marched away.

# Chapter Eight

Despite previously deciding not to, Kit was now bursting to tell Henry all that had happened to him since they last met; it was simply too good to keep to himself any longer. And wouldn't Henry's face be a picture? Kit smiled imagining his look of utter astonishment as he told him everything in a matter-of-fact, this-could-have-happened-to-anyone kind of way. But not tonight—tomorrow; for once Kit managed to act with patience. It wasn't that he thought twice about disturbing Henry's sleep at some black hour in the middle of the night (after all he had done that often enough before now!), it was that he sensed he was being followed through the palace—a flicker of shadow on the stairway convincing him he was right.

So the next morning after a pitiful breakfast of stale rolls, and cold coffee served up in a cracked cup, Kit hurried to Henry's room hoping to share a princely breakfast with him.

Walking briskly, his mind went over the previous day's events again and again. He felt he was coming close to the heart of the mystery, and there he should not be surprised to find Mr Skinner playing a very large part. Even Henry would have to admit it curious that Mr Skinner was out so late at night with a signalling lamp—in a city where he knew no one (or so he made out) and where the only ones around likely to see were the band of pretend enchanters. It was right that Kit should also tell his friend how he suspected Mr Skinner of working with that sly-looking girl, Tita, and how together they had tried to frighten him off.

The one real puzzle remaining was the gremlin, but the more Kit thought about it the more ready he was to admit that the creature glimpsed in the shadows wasn't Luddite. Couldn't have been. As he told himself, there was more than one gremlin at large in the world. Probably hundreds if they were all counted. Unfortunately that only raised another question. How did one come to be in Callalabasa, a land that forbids magic and therefore gremlins which are magical creatures . . . ? Kit couldn't come up with an even halfway reasonable answer and thinking about it gave him a headache. He shrugged.

'P'rhaps Henry can work it out,' he said brightly.

He hurried under an arch into a small courtyard filled with masses of garishly coloured flowers, their scent so overpowering that he stopped and wrinkled up his nose.

'Ah, Mr Stixby, you have found my secret little hiding place. Welcome—welcome. A pleasure to see you.'

Kit glanced to his side and saw Duke Liechenspit sitting cross-legged on a red tasselled cushion in the full glare of the sun. He was smoking a hookah and had taken the long flexible pipe from his mouth to speak, his words a slow outpouring of sound and smoke. Smiling, he sucked upon the pipe again and the hookah bubbled fiercely, a lazy wisp of smoke drifting from a corner of his lips.

'Oh,' Kit sounded disappointed. He had not meant to be rude, but he was so eager to get to Henry and tell him all his adventures that he could not bear to be side-tracked, even for a moment.

Duke Liechenspit didn't appear to notice. He rose from the cushion like a contented cat and straightened his fez.

'What news we awake to this morning,' he said with a gleam in his eye. 'Surely you must have heard, Mr Stixby?'

'Er . . . no,' said Kit.

The duke began to walk and it seemed impolite of Kit not to stroll along beside him, even though he didn't want to. He glanced helplessly over his shoulder—the duke was taking him in totally the wrong direction to the one he wanted.

Distracted, he grew aware of the duke talking again.

'Enchanters—those wicked devils—went on the rampage in the city last night, undoubtedly trying to spoil our coronation plans. Reports are still rather vague, but it seems they used their black arts to slip past the city gates and then poisoned many wells. How they must hate us and our new dear king.'

'But—' Kit opened his mouth to explain that the hooded riders weren't real enchanters—they were phoneys with absolutely nothing to do with magic; while this great show they presented *as magic* was in fact a handful of cheap tricks.

'Yes?'

Wisely Kit closed his mouth and said nothing.

Duke Liechenspit smiled. They turned into a cool cloister built of pure white stone, doves cooing in the splashes of bright sunshine.

'Of course I know what you are thinking,' continued the duke picking up on the silence.

'You do?' gasped Kit sincerely hoping he didn't.

'I do,' he said. 'You think in your country such barbaric acts are not possible . . . Ah, so civilized. But here magic is twisted into something worm infested and hateful; and the more it is driven underground the darker it becomes.'

He shook his head; doves settled behind them as they passed.

Growing more impatient, Kit decided to make an excuse and slip away.

'Sor—'

'It is not that the devils grow any less brazen with their magic,' said the duke cutting him off. 'Why, do you know, Mr Stixby, I have received reliable eye-witness accounts of one of these villains parading himself through the streets of Luca in broad daylight—daylight mark you—as bold as you and I, trying to bewitch our simple folk by passing himself off as a magical healer. Can you believe such a thing, Mr Stixby?'

'No,' mumbled Kit, his shoulders shifting uncomfortably inside his jacket.

'And that is only the half of it. Another of these unscrupulous fellows was seen to fly up from the city on a broomstick and invade the very walls of the palace.'

'*No* . . . I mean no wizard would dare do such a thing.'

The duke waved his hand. 'True, Mr Stixby, I'm afraid, I have seen the wretch's handiwork with my own eyes. The great clock is ruined—mindlessly vandalized beyond repair. Of course, I am not sentimental for old, worn-out things, but that is not the point.'

Kit realized the gremlin had been doing what it did best—destroying machinery. The duke went on—

'I suspect there'll also be a few curses left lying in wait, ready to trap an innocent passer-by. Well, we'll deal with them as they turn up. I only hope this wizard creature has taken himself off to some other place, because if he is still at the palace I pity him, I really do.'

'What do you mean?'

But Duke Liechenspit wasn't listening, he was gazing over Kit's head.

'Ah, I see the good archbishop is trying to attract my attention. I think he may need to go over a few details before the coronation ceremony tomorrow. If you would excuse me, Mr Stixby . . . '

Kit mumbled something, he didn't know what, and the duke flashed him a brilliant smile and was gone.

'Skinner!' uttered Kit in disgust and misery. 'I bet he did this to get even for his broken wireless. Must be him, who else was around to see me fly back into the palace? He's gone and dropped a word in someone's ear. 'Spect it suits his plans to have me stuck away in some ol' dungeon where I can't interfere no more but just rot away same as that funny old count I met yesterday.'

As he was saying this, plans were forming in his head—escape plans. He would tell Henry, Henry had to know, of course; then he must make his way as quickly as possible to the *Flying George*. Carpet should still be in the hold—unless . . . No, surely they wouldn't harm Carpet, Kit refused to consider any nasty possibilities here . . . On Carpet he could make a perfect getaway and wait across the border for Henry's return flight home, hopefully without Mr Skinner who would be in deep disgrace. Yes, let him be sent back to England in the smelly cargo-bay of a tramp cloud-clipper. That'll teach him. But first things first—

'Find Henry,' he said aloud in a determined voice.

However, on looking around, Kit realized he was in a part of the palace he did not recognize, in a room coolly tiled in blue and white, with walnut doors, and tall blue Chinese vases big enough to hide in and lidded like temple domes. He strode on hoping ever more desperately to turn a corner and find himself outside Henry's room. Yet much to his impatience every flight of steps directed him further downwards, deeper into the palace. He stopped several servants (who were less well dressed than those on the floors above). They simply couldn't understand him. One led him to a fountain and, grinning, gave him a drink of water.

'Stupid—stupid,' muttered Kit irritably. 'There ought

to be signs on the walls or summat, like road signs pointing the way.' He conveniently forgot that if there were they were not likely to be in English.

The dim corridors grew narrower and meaner, with little in the way of fine furniture (or furniture at all) and nothing on the walls except cheap wallpaper . . . and finally bare plaster. Kit sniffed. If the mildly unpleasant cabbagey smell was anything to go by he was very close to the kitchens.

Then all at once he heard a terrible commotion, raised voices and wailing; and as he stood wondering what it was, a great throng of people came into view—the lowest servants mostly, the potato peelers, boot polishers, soot collectors: those so low at the palace that none wore a uniform beyond a handed down hat or grubby apron. They were being driven along by members of the Magic Watch using whips and batons; Captain Slobbahn stuffing his face on a pig's trotter and wiping his greasy hands down his uniform.

Kit didn't realize the great danger he was in. Before he could think properly and prevent it happening, the pitiful throng overtook him and swept him up. Too late Kit saw he was caught as tightly as in a trap of steel. He didn't dare risk making a bolt for it for fear of drawing attention to himself and being recognized from the previous day. (And the guards were bound to remember him if he gave them half the chance.) So acting more calmly than he felt he pushed his way to the middle of the throng and kept his head down. Frightened, weeping people stumbled into him, and he wondered what on earth was going on.

Eventually the guards herded the people into a long plain windowless room, so stuffy that Kit could hardly breathe. Nothing was said for a time and the people cried less loudly, although they trembled and wrung their hands in fear. Everyone, including the Magic Watch, appeared to be waiting nervously for someone to arrive. Kit had no idea who nor why this mystery person should have such a powerful hold.

The waiting ended suddenly.

Startled, Kit jumped along with everyone else when the doors unexpectedly flew open and struck the wall with a resounding crash. Afterwards a tense silence settled thickly around them—so thick, indeed, that Kit felt he could reach out and touch it if only he dared move his hand. Those who needed to cry now muffled their sobs and whimpers; it was almost too unbearable.

Into the silence then came the sound of boots walking slowly across the floorboards. *Step . . . step . . . step . . .* Someone had entered who was used to commanding respect, and, as he advanced, no one, not even Captain Slobbahn, was brave enough to look him in the eye. *Step . . . step . . . step . . .* The newcomer placed himself squarely before them all, a heavy, fur collared coat slung over his broad shoulders, hands on hips, waiting his moment.

And then he sniffed.

And what a sniff, it sounded like the first stirrings of a hurricane. Astonished, Kit glanced up to see the biggest nose he had ever seen in all his life. It was simply enormous; and the coarse dense sprouts of nose hair that flourished in both cavernous nostrils trembled like black twigs in a storm, as the man sucked in and filled up his lungs.

And then he stopped, nodded appreciatively to his audience, and dabbed his brow with a handkerchief like an opera singer who had just finished a particularly taxing aria.

Kit shuddered. He had heard about men like this. Most Excellent Noses they called themselves, although the nickname *Sniffers* was a less flattering title. Either way, they were so called for their ability to smell out magic.

One of the Magic Watch brought a stool and the Sniffer glowered at it savagely, his dense eyebrows rising and his eyes lighting up like the villain's in a touring melodrama. The guard stammered his humblest apologies and backed away, returning with a heavy, cushioned chair. His most Excellent Nose, Señor Pufni, flung his coat across its back and sat watching the guards use their batons and whips to drive the poor servants into line; Kit, amongst them, kept his head down and pressed his hands to his eyes, making sure his face stayed hidden. But he could hardly see where he was going. Roughly someone jostled their way in beside him, but he was far too busy worrying to bother to see who.

'I . . . can . . . smell . . . MAGIC!' roared Señor Pufni with a flourish of a stunningly large handkerchief.

'The stench of magic is *here*,' he boomed. 'It fills my senses. Yes—yes, I smell it in the air like rotting flesh, like a cesspit in high summer; foul enough to turn away the dung beetle and crawling maggot—to make a sewer rat sick. It taints us all with its filth!'

Captain Slobbahn approached him and bowed, nervously running a greasy hand up and down his thigh.

'S-Señor Pufni, please, if you would be so good. We have them lined up ready for inspection. Take your time. Just walk along and point out the stinking polecat who offends your delicate nose.'

'Very well, Captain, if I must.'

Señor Pufni sighed and rose with the look of weary indifference. He began at the far end of the line, sniffing in deeply as he inched his way along.

Kit stared helplessly at his feet, his whole body trembled.

Content to take his time, the Sniffer moved slowly nearer. Waiting became an agony. 'The stench grows stronger!' he declared with a dramatic roar, making several women shriek hysterically.

This is it for sure, thought Kit. He'll smell fresh magic all over me, he's bound to—there's nothing I can do. *Nothin'*. And I'll never go home ever again—

'And stronger still. My stomach heaves!'

Briefly it did occur to Kit to use his magic: to fire his way out of this with both hands blazing. But in the end where would it get him? He saw he was greatly outnumbered by the Watch and, just when he needed it most, he felt his flame of magic guttering inside him, half snuffed out by the knots in his stomach.

The Sniffer flashed his dark eyes. 'I feel the fumes of The Pit gathering around me,' he said in a low rumbling voice. 'Clouds of brimstone . . . choking smoke . . . But be assured, little devil, you will be forced out into the light. I will force you into the revealing glare of the sun.'

Suddenly overcome, he paused and trumpeted his nose on his tablecloth sized handkerchief. The air quivered. He was only a few steps down the line from Kit. Discovery lay seconds away.

Kit waited. A shadow fell across him. He squeezed his eyes shut so tight they hurt. A long intake of air . . . Then he heard the Sniffer slowly speak.

'Gentlemen, the vile creature is unmasked . . . '

Kit's knees nearly gave way in fright. Señor Pufni made a grab.

'Let me go! Let me go!'

Kit's eyes jerked open and he stared in amazement. The Sniffer had seized the person *next to him*—the same one who had deliberately pushed in beside him. Her long dark hair whipped across her face as she struggled. Roughly she was dragged away by the Watch; followed out of the room by Señor Pufni, his handkerchief pressed firmly to his face as though about to be sick.

Kit stared after them, dumbstruck.

The girl who had been arrested was Tita.

But . . . that could only mean one thing. The words came slowly out of a fog of confusion.

'Tita is a witch!'

# Chapter Nine

'And you are sure she stood next to you on purpose so *she* would be found out instead of you?' asked Henry. He slid a box of Turkish Delight across his mammoth sized bed at Kit.

Kit shook his head. He couldn't even think about eating anything now. He was still feeling rather shaken up by his narrow escape. On top of all else he had suddenly and surprisingly grown extremely concerned for Tita, imagining her locked away in some dark hole in the dungeon deep below them.

Henry shrugged, pulled back the box and helped himself to the largest piece he could see, dropping sugar on the silk counterpane.

'Think about it,' said Kit. 'If you were Tita, at that moment you would be the only person in the whole world to know there were two enchanters in the room, so it would be easy as anything to save yourself. All you needed to do was keep your head down and get a place at the far end of the line away from the first enchanter—me in other words—and make sure the Sniffer smelt him out first.'

'Doesn't make sense,' said Henry, his mouth stuffed.

'I know—nothing does. You think you understand something then summat else happens and everything turns back to being as clear as prize-winning London fog. If Tita *is* a witch, why does she hang around with a well known magic-hater like Ernest Skinner? And don't forget only she had time to leave that warning in my room when we first arrived. I saw her come out the door.'

Henry reached out his hand but changed his mind and took it back with a groan. 'Ugh, I think I may have over done it on the Turkish Delight.'

'Serves you right, greedy pig,' said Kit unsympathetically.

Henry put the box away and licked the sugary crumbs off his fingers. 'There is one way of finding out all you wanted to know,' he said absently. 'You could send your mind down into the dungeon and ask the girl straight out for the truth.'

Kit stared at him.

'What have I said?' asked Henry alarmed.

'Nothin'—you're an absolute genius that's all, Henry. Why didn't I think of that?'

'Turkish Delight,' said Henry modestly. 'Perfect brain food.'

Henry took charge at once. He rushed about busily plumping up cushions to make his bed as comfortable as possible for Kit's body while his mind was out walking. As he fussed around excitedly, he didn't notice Kit turn quiet and doubtful.

Kit chewed the side of his thumb.

'Henry,' he began slowly. 'What d'you think the dungeon'll be like? . . . Do you think it'll be horrible? Do you think . . . ' his voice sank to a whisper, 'they still might actually torture people down there with thumbscrews and racks and hot pokers and stuff?'

Henry paused. 'Hadn't thought of that,' he admitted. 'You could possibly be right, it is a dungeon, after all, and it's a well known fact that dungeons have torture chambers . . . You know, Kit, if you change your mind and don't send it I wouldn't blame you one little bit.'

'I didn't say I wouldn't send it,' snapped Kit. 'Whatever else, Tita deserves our help. If it wasn't for her

I would be there in person finding out the truth for myself. Now don't disturb me, Henry, and go see that the door is locked and no one can come in. If Mr Skinner comes by, say you have a bad headache and need to lie down in a dark room. If he asks, tell him you have no idea where I am.'

'Well, I won't,' grinned Henry. 'At least not part of you.'

Kit lay on the bed and closed his eyes; his mind rose up out of him and drifted phantom-like from the room and along the corridor. Thereafter, whenever it reached a flight of stairs it chose to go down it—down towards the dungeon. But finding what it wanted wasn't easy. Several times it wound up in dead end storerooms and once in the king's dusty wine cellar. Henry noticed Kit's eyelids flicker in frustration.

Finally his mind arrived at a rough-cut archway with a lighted torch upon either side. Beyond the opening, stairs spiralling down had been worn smooth by the passing of many feet (dragged down them in some instances) and were so steep and twisting that a rusted chain was fixed to the wall to act as a handrail. Not that Kit's mind had use for anything so crude and clumsy: it flowed down the stairwell with the ease of a glow-ball and came to a halt at the bottom. Kit knew at once this was the dungeon, he sensed it from the troubled darkness. He grew uneasy. Fearful echoes from down the centuries rippled around him. Cracked and ghostly voices crept from the stones, leaking out like the damp which made the air so unwholesome.

Hesitantly he began to call.

*Tita? Tita?*

No one answered, so he pressed on and searched amongst the cells. He was surprised to find them empty. He must have gone through at least ten and was close to despair, when he come across one that *did* have a prisoner inside.

*This way—this way*, he was urged by an excited voice. *Come in. Please, come in.*

As soon as Kit entered he knew he had made a grave mistake. He found himself in a brain so cunning it resembled an ever-changing maze, the walls like dazzling mirrors reflecting themselves; and it struck him so utterly cold that back in Henry's room his body shivered violently. Poor Henry, not knowing what else to do, wrapped him up in every coat and blanket he could find.

More controlled now and sounding oddly familiar, the voice spoke to Kit in a purr.

*Ah, well now, the little English boy. Welcome. I am happy to have you visit, though perhaps a little sad that it is not I who am the real reason for you paying this call.*

*C-Count Drohlomski.*

*Indeed. I half guessed you had wizardly powers when we met yesterday . . . Call it a gift I have. Although, alas, not a wizard myself I pride myself on having certain insights, and I recognized there was something more in you. I was right, wasn't I? So perhaps there is a streak of magic in me after all. A darker magic than yours, I fancy.*

Kit instinctively shrank back from him, remembering his long yellow nails; but the count was all around, circling him, making him feel dizzy.

*I don't want this to sound rude or nothin' but I can't stay. I'm looking for a girl called Tita, the one who was arrested this morning by the Magic Watch.*

*You enchanters*, said the count amused and mocking. *You always take such good care of each other. So touching, so moving. Ha-ha. I could squeeze out a tear.*

*Then you can tell me where she is—I mean, which cell she's in?*

101

*I can tell you exactly where she is, English boy, but she is not in any cell.*

**Where is she?**

The count paused, taking delicious pleasure from each lingering moment. *Like any of her—aah—your kind, she is being taken to the Forest of Tungol. Such a charming place especially at this time of the year, I for one can recommend—*

**Why?** demanded Kit.

Again the smiling, gloating pause. *It is our ancient way of dealing with enchanters. Quite exquisite really. There is a hunt and your little friend Tita will play the part of the fox.*

**A witch-hunt!** gasped Kit. *But that's terrible. I didn't think they happened these days. I must go—I must do what I can to help her.*

**How? You are here with me . . . my precious little pet, my bright jewel, my innocent lamb . . .**

For the first time Kit became aware of an icy web around his mind, growing rapidly like a crystal of ice, pressing against him as it grew. The count chuckled in a self-satisfied way.

In truth he disgusted Kit more than anything, but Kit still managed to remain polite towards him. *Thank you for telling me what I wanted to know, Count*, he said briskly. *I have to go now.*

He felt the count's cold powerful mind trying to block him in, the cunning paths of the maze growing more complex around him; its grip tightening, squeezing the very life out of him.

**Now see here, you withered old windbag!** stormed Kit in an outburst of frightened anger, and flying up like an agitated bird he beat hard against the count's skull; he did it again and again until he heard the count groan and felt his hold suddenly slacken.

Relieved more than he could say, Kit's mind raced from the dungeon and up the stairs; it did not slow down until it had reached Henry's room and was safely back home. He opened his eyes to Henry's reassuring face.

'That was close,' he said blowing out his cheeks.

It was clear to Kit that the only way left to help Tita now was by magic. If he was to follow her to the Forest of Tungol, which he had every intention of doing, the best and most obvious way was by flying-carpet.

'Well, if you go I'm coming with you,' said Henry forcibly. 'It's not fair, you've already had ten times more adventure than me. Why should *I* be left behind when you have your next one?'

Kit saw by the look on his face how determined he was. It was not a look to be argued with. Still, he did try—

'But it means breaking the law and you're a prince, Henry—' He smiled. '—although sometimes perhaps not a very proper one. And what about ol' Mr Skinner?'

'*Pah!* to silly laws and *Pah!* to being a prince. *Pah!* to Mr Skinner too if he were around to hear it, but I haven't seen him since yesterday. Are you ready to go yet or are we going to waste even more time arguing?'

Kit's smile widened. 'Yeah, I'm ready,' he said.

He patted Henry on the back.

'What?' said Henry still fierce.

'Oh, nothing,' replied Kit, although he couldn't help feeling glad that Henry was his best friend.

As they left the palace and hurried through the streets of Luca, Kit kept glancing over his shoulder, the habit hard to break. He was sure Mr Skinner wasn't following them and was glad of that, of course, but it made him wonder why not, after all Mr Skinner had less reason to trust him

103

now than ever before—and rightfully so. And while he was in such a thoughtful mood, he wondered if Mr Skinner realized that Tita was a witch; Kit couldn't imagine for a minute he did; but then what was the point of Tita keeping it from him—or, for that matter, ever helping him in the first place? These were questions he must ask her when he had the chance.

Without the detective around, getting away from the palace had proved ridiculously easy. In the corridor they had also the good fortune to run into Dummock, and Henry unashamedly told him a bare-faced lie. He said that he and Kit had been invited to tea at the castle of the Countess Von Biffbumburg and if it grew too late they would stay overnight.

'Countess what?' Kit had laughed on the way down in the wicker basket.

'*Biffbumburg*, it's the first name I could think up on the spot and rather good it is too,' said Henry proudly. 'It certainly impressed Dummock and at least he won't worry if he can't find me at the palace. He's rather dramatic as you know. The last thing I want is him raising the alarm and then leaving me to answer a lot of awkward questions.'

'I bet Mr Skinner'll see through your false countess in a second,' said Kit. 'I bet he'll know you've been up to summat—and prob'ly summat with me.'

'Mr Skinner can think what he likes,' replied Henry pretending to play the haughty prince. 'But if he dares to say anything I shall point out that he has failed in his duty as my bodyguard. He should have been here to stop me falling into wicked ways with bad company. Oh, that's you by the way, Kit.'

Kit pushed him playfully. 'So I'm your whipping-boy now am I?'

'Of course, it's all you're really good for.'

The sun was very hot. In the narrow streets it didn't matter so much, with the shadows from the awnings cooling them, but out on the open road without a single tree to cast its shade, the sun blazed fiery and red, and orange dust blew into their faces.

Kit wished he'd worn a hat, it was too hot to think. Before him through a shimmering heat haze he glimpsed the airships moored to the ruined tower. They rippled like silk flags. And while it needed no effort to spot them, reaching them was a different matter. He and Henry trudged in silence through the mid-day heat. Dust stuck to their sticky faces; and Kit briefly wondered what might be happening to Tita at that exact moment beneath the same blazing sun; several unpleasant ideas made him forget his own discomfort and walk just that little bit faster.

At long last they reached the tower. Two Callalabasian soldiers stood on sentry duty at the doorway; oddly they appeared to be sharing a single old-fashioned uniform between them—one wearing the dented helmet, the other the jacket; one having the boots and one the trousers. On seeing Kit and Henry, both men reached at the same time for an ancient blunderbuss propped against the wall, the one who seized it first frowning at the other as if declaring it was *his* turn with the weapon. They saluted as the boys went by, through the doorway and up the stairs.

Aboard the *Flying George* a small crew of five were left to look after the daily running of the ship. They were cheerful and friendly, but apart from that didn't pay the boys much attention. Henry stuffed his pockets with apples and filled a flask with drinking water; Kit slipped away to the hold. He entered nervously, but was relieved to find Carpet exactly as he had left it.

'Carpet?' he whispered and it perked up at once.

Their reunion made Kit's magic glow with happiness, after all a wizard without the means to fly is as incomplete as a cowboy without a horse. Carpet was no less overjoyed. It went slightly loopy, finding as many different ways of wrapping itself around Kit as it could, nearly sweeping him off his feet. After several unsuccessful attempts, Kit finally managed to roll it up and tuck it under his arm. He was forced to speak to it quite sternly.

'For heaven's sake stop wrigglin', Carpet, or you'll give the game away before we even start,' he hissed.

He met Henry at the main disembarking gangplank, a smile enough to tell him all was well. Then they went down past the two Callalabasian guards, Kit casually carrying Carpet as if it were a perfectly commonplace object to carry back in England—like an umbrella or walking-stick. The sentries saluted, Kit noting that this time the other one had charge of the gun.

Once out of sight the two friends headed for a small spinney of ancient gnarled pines, the ground about their roots littered with fallen cones.

'Down to business,' said Kit, throwing open Carpet at Henry's feet.

Hurriedly they took up their places amongst the half faded patterns; Kit leaned forward to give his flying orders.

'Fast and straight this time, Carpet,' he said. 'And that means none of your usual showy stuff to please the crowds. In fact it's far better if no one sees us at all—so jus' you concentrate on following the forest road and getting us to Tungol as quickly as you can. Well, what are you waiting for? Go!'

With a rush of air Carpet jumped off the ground and they were flying, scooting over little yew bushes and catching and snapping off the dead end twigs of the bigger trees. Then, with hardly a sound except for the wind roaring in their ears, Carpet rose vertically, its back stepped to prevent its two riders from sliding off. Kit gripped Carpet's fringed edges, but before he could gasp it abruptly levelled off and below him lay Callalabasa spread out and revealed like a finely detailed map, giving him and Henry an angel-eyed view right to its borders and the lands beyond. Ahead, Kit noticed mountains, their shoulders and feet dark with trees. He pointed and Henry nodded in agreement. The Forest of Tungol.

Soon Carpet started to spiral down on a fresh mountain breeze—and not a moment too soon. In the distance on a dusty forest track appeared a procession of horsemen and hounds, some horsemen riding before and some riding behind a rumbling cart built like a cage on solid wheels. Inside the cage a frightened girl cowered in a corner, half hidden by a heap of dirty straw; straw clinging to her long dark hair.

And, as Kit and Henry watched, the cart went over a pothole and the girl fell forward onto her face, her hands bound behind her so she could not help herself—and certainly not with magic. Besides, even with her hands free, Kit knew how fear ate away at an enchanter's power. Right now he'd be surprised if Tita's magic added up to a ha'p'orth's worth of gunpowder.

He ordered Carpet to fly down. 'Unseen,' he said.

On reaching the forest canopy, Carpet sank through a green sea of leaves and shadowed the riders, sprinting forward from tree to tree to avoid detection.

'Look,' said Kit bleakly. 'There's Alecu Slobhahn, captain of the Magic Watch.'

Kit recognized and pointed out to Henry a number of his men. They were grim and silent, swatting away the troublesome mosquitoes.

Then a rider came thundering back along the track. Dressed in smart hunting pink and with a whip beneath his arm, he looked to all the world like a fine fox hunting gentleman.

Kit scowled the moment he saw the tight black bowler hat.

'Skinner!' he said in disgust.

# Chapter Ten

Skinner reined up hard beside Captain Slobbahn.

'Captain,' he said, 'might I suggest we get the hunt under way as quickly as possible. If we go much deeper into the forest I doubt we shall be back at the palace in time for supper.'

The captain grunted and scratched his whiskery chin. Whether Mr Skinner knew it or not, the thought of missing out on a meal made a powerful argument in his favour. Captain Slobbahn nodded and roared out the order to stop. Two men were sent to fetch Tita. As they dismounted, Kit thought, I've seen those black horses before. They're the ones ridden by the pretend enchanters. One mystery solved then . . .

Tita was dragged from her cage and made to stand trembling before Mr Skinner and the members of the Magic Watch.

'Well, witch,' said Mr Skinner disdainfully. 'The custom may be new to me but I'm sure I need not remind you of how it must be, this being the penalty paid by all those who practise your filthy art. You will be given ten minutes to make your way wherever you please, after that the hunt begins; and like all hunts it will not end until blood is drawn or the quarry escapes. Do you understand?'

Tita nodded and glanced around at their leering faces. 'Sir,' she whispered, 'my hands . . . won't you loosen the rope a little?'

Mr Skinner laughed scornfully. 'What, so you can slip

free of them and attack us with your witchcraft. Do we look like complete idiots?'

Captain Slobbahn belched and scratched deep in his armpit. Mr Skinner took out a pocket watch and studied the second-hand carefully. 'Your time, witch, begins . . . now!'

Henry and Kit watched in silence, seeing Tita run scared for a little way along the forest track, then throw herself into a dense thicket; having no hands to fend them away, the branches clawed at her face and hair. Captain Slobbahn and his men jeered and made cruel remarks.

'Dirty, smelly old bullies!' said Kit fierce enough for tears. He beat down his fist on Carpet. 'It isn't fair, Henry. There's so many of them and they have sabres and horses and dogs.'

'Getting angry's not going to help the poor girl,' said Henry calmly. 'And don't forget we have magic on our side. Come on, we've got to join the hunt and pray we can find her first.'

Kit knew he was right. He ordered Carpet to move steadily through the woodland, making a wide circle around the huntsmen; telling it to cross the track behind them where there was less likelihood of being seen.

Rippling forward like a gentle gust of wind, Carpet slipped around tree trunks and under fallen branches and through trailing curtains of ivy. It moved so stealthily that forest creatures were taken by surprise—squirrels fleeing chattering in terror, their fur standing on end. Kit felt so tense he never gave them a second glance.

'Five minutes!' they heard Mr Skinner shout, his voice helping to give them their bearings. But then Carpet got lost. No longer could they hear voices or the sound of the huntsmen's animals, and the track never reappeared. Kit grew madly impatient.

'Left here—no, right. Stars' teeth! Why can't we see

past these trees? Oh, come on, Carpet—is it asking too much for you to get more of a move on?'

'Stop!' cried Henry suddenly. Kit glared at him but this time Henry was giving the orders. 'Carpet, I want you to go back through the forest to where we first started.'

Carpet hesitated.

'Go ahead, do it,' said Kit sulkily.

With a definite destination in mind and a remembered path to follow, Carpet zoomed back at a speed some might consider reckless. Birds flew up squawking in alarm, and even Henry gulped a few times as one moment they tilted around a tree and the next exploded through a wall of leaves.

Seconds later Carpet jerked to a halt. Kit and Henry once more had a clear view of the forest track, only now they discovered it was deserted.

'Oh no,' cried Kit. 'The hunt is under way! Quickly, Carpet, give us some height.'

The flying-carpet effortlessly climbed a hundred feet into the sky. An ocean of shimmering green opened out before them. Without a breeze the topmost branches moved so little that they could hardly be described as swaying; even so, away to the left they saw a patch of forest that surged violently, the movement accompanied by the snapping of branches and ripping of leaves.

Kit ordered Carpet to fly closer.

Carpet was above the scene almost before he'd finished speaking. Peering down through the branches, Kit glimpsed horsemen hacking their way forward with sabres, cursing loudly whenever a briar snagged a jacket or scored a bloody scratch on a face. Kit nodded approvingly.

'Exactly what I'd do if I were Tita,' he said. 'Lead 'em a merry dance through the densest part of the forest. It's bound to slow them down and win more time.'

'But not the pack,' Henry reminded him.

111

That was true. At one stage Henry reckoned that the hounds' ancestors had been crossed with wolves. They were large, coarse-haired, scrawny things with red-rimmed eyes and soft floppy jowls. And on top of an unfortunate appearance they were probably half starved, for like any neglected animal they were slavishly anxious to please and desperate in their hope for some scrap of affection in return, a kind word or pat—or better still, a bone to chew over. Lean and agile, they were able to go wherever Tita went, but twice as swiftly and with half the effort.

Kit put himself in Tita's place wondering what *he* might do. Throw the dogs off his scent seemed the most sensible idea; but the question was how—magic was impossible. He frowned as he thought . . . *Water*. That's it! Dogs can't follow a quarry's scent through water. Looking up quickly, Kit caught the gleam of a wide forest lake. Clever old Tita, he thought, even with her hands tied behind her she would have powers enough to sense it there.

'We'll fly to the lake and meet her on the shore,' he whooped.

Racing ahead of the hunt, Carpet reached the lake and hovered over the shallows. It was a perfect place. Little crystal waves washed over smooth round pebbles and speckled fish edged slowly amongst the deep sun-lit crevices. It was altogether so calm and peaceful there, especially when compared to the forest, where trees surged and snapped as in a hurricane. Absently Kit picked at Carpet's fringe. It looked to him as if the hunt was heading directly their way. 'Hurry, Tita, hurry,' Henry muttered behind him.

They heard the bark of excited hounds growing louder and more distantly the roars of men. Then suddenly the green wall of foliage along the water's edge burst open and Tita staggered into view, bloody and exhausted, her hands still tied behind her.

'Down!' yelped Kit the instant she appeared for he saw she was not alone. With the ease of two grey shadows, a pair of scrawny hounds had slipped free of the forest and pausing only to shake the twigs and leaves from their coats were after her in great bounding strides, their lips drawn back and fangs gleaming.

And then the trees by the waterside began their tremendous shaking and thrashing again, only this time much more violently than before so that Kit wondered briefly if they were possessed by a wild uncontrollable magic—but then the answer became revealed. A dense thicket suddenly split apart scattering leaves madly; from the centre of it Captain Slobbahn rode out upon the lake's shore having bulldozed his way through branch and briar; his poor punished horse cut, his uniform shredded, and his cap snatched off his head by twigs. But none of this mattered to him: his expression pure evil, he lifted his well polished sabre high above his head and spurred his horse forward.

Carpet swooped like a hawk, the air turning dark and blurred at its corners. Sitting cross-legged on its back, Kit awaited the right moment: his hand was risen and he closed one eye taking careful aim down the length of his arm. Magic flared up inside him eager to serve, the next instant he unleashed it through his fingers. A ball of brilliant white light went speeding before him, spilling sparks as it went. The light struck the sabre's blade causing an even brighter flash. Captain Slobbahn howled and jerked back his burnt hand, his sabre rattling along the ground—black and smoking and practically bent double.

But now more worryingly the pebbly beach appeared on course to hit them like a solid wall. Behind him Kit heard Henry suck in his breath, yet he himself was unafraid. He knew Carpet was an experienced acrobat. He trusted it completely. Sure enough, inches away from disaster, Carpet pulled out of its dive and with all the speed it had mustered went flying low over the hounds, so low in fact that the ragged fur along their backs sprang up like flames. This confused the creatures into a kind of madness and they spun round and round until they were dizzy.

'Here, Tita—hurry!'

Kit and Henry shouted at the tops of their voices. They knew they didn't have long and that their moment of surprise was fast fading. Already Captain Slobbahn was struggling with a painfully blistered hand to unclip his holster and pull out his revolver. He looked murderous enough to put a bullet into all three of them.

Tita stood confused in the middle not able to decide her friends (if any) from her enemies. Then all at once she made up her mind. She hurled herself at Carpet which hovered a few feet off the ground in front of her. Henry and Kit grabbed her legs and hauled her aboard.

'Away, Carpet!' shouted Kit.

Heavier and clumsier than before, it rose. Captain Slobbahn waved his revolver in the air. A puff of dirty smoke appeared at its barrel; a split second later a bang was heard and a bullet whistled by at a harmless distance . . . And soon the captain was no more than a tiny figure on the shore.

Safe on board Carpet as it circled high above the lake, an awkward silence fell amongst the three youngsters now the danger which had bound them so tightly was left simmering harmlessly below. And as Kit was wondering what to say, Tita turned to him, her face pale and spattered with dirt.

'Thank you, both of you. You saved my life,' she said in a fierce whisper.

Kit studied her. 'Think of it as returning a favour,' he

said, unable to resist adding, 'A favour from one enchanter to another.' And he grinned at her.

'Yes,' Tita nodded then grinned back in relief.

Henry took out his penknife and cut her hands free.

'Where to now?' he asked as practical as ever. 'We can't very well return to the palace and goodness knows what row all this will lead to when it finally catches up with us.'

Rubbing her sore wrists, Tita nodded across the lake. 'Fly on towards the mountains,' she said. 'I will show you a place—a special place you will hardly believe. In your language it is called Mountain Tree. But it is protected by so many spells that your flying-carpet will never find it from the air. I will show you only if you promise never to breathe a word of it to anyone, not even its name. There is a power in names even to those who don't have magic.'

Kit and Henry both solemnly promised—Gang honour—if only because it sounded so intriguing. Then Kit set a course for the tallest mountain peak in the range before them and Tita nodded her approval. Once this was sorted out, she was at last free to examine her scratches and bruises of which she certainly had quite a few—not that she once complained and Kit admired her for that, and for the way she quietly set about removing marks and stings with a touch of her finger.

Carpet meanwhile flew on across the silver lake, not meeting a moment's turbulence and as well it didn't. It was noticeably less stable with three people on board. Feeling content with himself, Kit peered over the side to watch his reflection in the still, steely grey waters. Ahead, the sun was sinking behind the mountains; and once they reached the forest on the far side the shadows cast by the jagged peaks made it feel much cooler.

'Land us here,' said Tita pointing at a clearing.

Carpet came down with a soft bump and its passengers climbed off.

'We go on foot from here,' Tita informed them. 'I know it seems a lot of bother, but believe me it will be much easier in the end. I suggest you either carry your carpet or tell it to follow behind.'

'But which way?' asked Kit.

Tita shrugged. 'I don't know, I'm not sure yet. I have to find a friendly tree to ask.'

'Did I hear right? Did she actually say *ask a tree*?' Henry whispered to Kit as they moved off; Carpet following riderless at their heels.

'You know, I believe she did,' said Kit smiling at Henry's incredulous expression. 'Why don't you ask her?'

'I shall,' said Henry. 'Er, Tita,' he called, 'just what exactly will you ask this useful tree of yours when you find it?'

'Where the paths are,' she answered, not turning back.

'What paths?'

'The paths leading to Mountain Tree, of course. What else? Now are we going to stand here talking all day or are you going to help?'

'Just tell us what to do,' said Kit good-naturedly.

She paused, looking around. 'Find a tree that is different. One that has moss growing on the south-facing side of its trunk.' She didn't explain why.

They searched together. The oaks in that part of the forest were countless years old, but alike in one respect: moss grew thickly on them but only on the north-facing sides of their branches and trunks; and after half an hour of searching it seemed unlikely they would find one in any way different.

'I can't work out how this is going to help us in any case,' grumbled Henry, keeping his voice low so Tita wouldn't hear.

116

'To be honest nor can I,' agreed Kit. 'All the trees are the same to me, it's sending me cross-eyed.'

Suddenly Tita gave a triumphant cry. 'Over here—I've found one!' And when they raced across to her they saw a tree unlike the others in exactly the way she said it would be, the moss thick and green on its sheltered southern side and nowhere else upon it.

'Now for some magic,' said Tita.

She found a stick as long and straight as a wand and scratched some symbols about its gnarled roots. Kit watched her, not understanding what they meant but knowing magic runes when he saw them. Resting her hand against its ancient trunk, Tita leant forward to speak to the tree; softly she murmured the words of an enchantment. When she finished, the tree's answer was instant and beautiful. A silvery path shining from deep underground, beginning at its roots and leading into the distance, glowing in the twilight like a strayed moonbeam.

Smiling delightedly, Tita stepped onto it; Henry followed, leading with his toe as if afraid he'd discover the magic path breathtakingly cold like a mountain stream, or so delicate it would shatter beneath his weight like glass.

Tita turned, saw him and laughed.

Kit followed Henry, marvelling at the ancientness of the magic. In England he had heard that Druids had used something very similar called moon paths or ley lines.

'Come on,' called Tita. 'We have a long walk ahead of us before we are there.'

The shining path wound through the forest, skirting other trees for about five hundred paces, until it ended at the roots of a second equally aged oak, which again had moss growing on its southern side and not the more usual north-facing side. Now he was aware of it, Kit saw what

117

an obvious marker this was, but to somebody else, somebody not looking for this difference, it would pass completely unnoticed.

Tita spoke to the tree with the same deep respect she would show to an elderly grandparent. The tree responded with kindness. Kit felt the air tingle and the next section of pathway was revealed to them. And it went on in this manner from special tree to special tree, running crookedly and ever upwards, around boulders and through fast flowing streams, lighting up the transparent water and the little fish that darted for cover. And whenever they left a section of pathway, it vanished immediately so they knew no one could follow.

Beneath the shadow of the trees night arrived swiftly. They pressed on without need of a lantern or glow-ball, and with the moon hopelessly lost in a tangle of twigs above their heads. And the darker it grew the clearer became the pathway, glowing fuzzy at the edges, throwing splashes of pale blue light onto the spreading limbs of the trees. And the strange thing was neither Kit nor Henry felt in the least bit tired despite climbing steeply at times. They guessed this was magic. Magic lay soft underfoot.

And Kit strongly suspected the path of making them invisible too.

The reason he thought this was the forest animals— they behaved as if no one was there. At one point a snowy white owl silently swooped out of the darkness between him and Henry, somehow managing to miss them both with only inches to spare upon either side. Deer, foxes, and badgers were commonplace companions. Yet Kit had to admit his hair stood on end slightly when a fully grown troll burst through the bushes and stared right through him with its tiny incredibly stupid eyes; it blinked, shook its dusty head, then lumbered off dragging a spiked club in one paw and a dead stag in the other.

Kit laughed, more from nervousness than anything else. 'Think what fun the gang back home could have with a magic path like this, eh, Henry.'

'*Shh!*' Tita turned and looked severe, a finger to her lips.

'What is it?'

'The gateway to Mountain Tree,' she replied.

'But it sounds like a waterfall,' said Henry.

'And so it is.'

# Chapter Eleven

The path left the forest and ran along a rocky cliff face to a gorge. On the other side thundered the waterfall. It began some fifty feet higher and broke unseen (though heard—yes, heard very loudly) upon rocks in a pit of darkness deep below their feet.

The air was wet and flecked with spray; ferns thrived, sprouting thickly among the crevices, and fat mounds of moss squelched underfoot. To be there felt very much like being caught in a dull November drizzle—London drizzle at that—and both Kit and Henry were quickly wet through, the water cold enough to make them shiver in their thin summer clothes.

At the place where the latest section of glowing path ended and the gorge began, stood a heavy boulder roughly hewn into the shape of a ball. It balanced precariously on a point, and to Kit's mind all it needed was half a breath of wind to set it rolling. Tita, however, rested her hands on the top and spoke to it, her voice harsher—necessarily so; this, after all, was stone not venerable wood. The boulder began to glow deep inside, the light swimming up to the surface. From this, two things happened at the very same time.

A bridge of light grew out from the boulder and across the gorge in a colourless rainbow; and, as it did, the tumbling waters drew aside for it like a living curtain. Behind it lay a ledge and a small arched opening.

Tita crossed the bridge first to show them they had nothing to fear; Kit followed and finally Henry, nervously edging his way forward—far less confident than his friends in the ways of magic. He looked very happy to jump down on the opposite side.

Oddly, the arch was completely dry and upon either side of it crouched a stone gorgon, fearsome looking creatures if ever there were, and so lifelike that Kit swore the eyes of the nearest one swivelled to take him in with a hostile stare. This perhaps explained why Tita hurriedly stepped forward and spoke to them, reassuring each one like a dutiful watchdog; ordering them to stay their ground and not see anyone off. Then she turned to Kit.

'Roll up your carpet and leave it here if you like,' she said. 'It'll be far safer and, well, I'd hate for you to lose it . . . It wouldn't be the first flying-carpet to be carried off by a moth.'

'A moth!' said Kit scornfully as he rolled up Carpet and stashed it behind one of the gorgons (did he hear a hiss?). 'I'd like to see the moth that could lift a flying-carpet.'

'You don't think it's possible?' replied Tita, her eyes sparkling and full of knowing. Saying no more on that particular matter she held out a hand gesturing through the dark archway. 'Welcome to Mountain Tree,' she said.

Through the opening, in a deep shadowy cleft in a mountainside, stood a single tree—an oak tree so timelessly old that its grey trunk had come to resemble a strange twisted rock formation; and only its leaves, green and abundant, showed that it still possessed life.

'A *tree* in a *mountain*,' said Henry disappointedly, perhaps hoping for something altogether more wonderful. '*Mountain Tree* . . . I don't know why I thought it could be anything else.'

Tita smiled her same knowing smile (or irritating as Kit now thought it). 'I'll go first,' she said, adding mysteriously, 'See you both down there.' And she strode off under the arch.

Hearing a sudden thunderous roar, Henry and Kit turned to glance over their shoulders. The curtain of water was falling back into place, tumbling across to hide its secret.

Fearful of a second wetting they hurried after Tita— only Tita was no longer there.

'That's funny, I wonder where she's—' Kit was saying when the air around him suddenly throbbed with intensely powerful magic; his ears popped and his wild hair bristled. The sensation lasted only a matter of seconds. Afterwards, although nothing appeared to have altered in any great way (and turning to look at Henry next to him only confirmed this), Kit knew somehow it must have done.

Henry, unused to big doses of magic, swayed dizzily as if he had just stepped off the wildest fairground ride ever invented. His hand slowly rose and he pointed long before the words would come.

'Look, Kit—look at the tree!' he at last managed to gasp.

Kit did and was instantly as awstruck as Henry. The tree had grown—more than grown, it had rocketed into the size of a mountain. Then the truth struck him. The tree hadn't changed at all, not by a single leaf . . . *They* were the ones who were changed, *he and Henry*. It must have been the arch. The arch had shrunk them to little more than half an inch. It was a shocking thought to consider but Kit was now the same size as his smallest toe—or rather, the size his smallest toe *used* to be.

Hearing Tita laugh, he spun round on his heels. 'That's why you warned me to leave Carpet behind,' he cried excitedly. 'Prob'ly a moth here'll seem the size of a—I dunno—an airship or summat!'

'They wouldn't mean any real harm though,' said Tita

clearly very fond of moths however big they were. 'You see, creatures that live naturally on the oak are their rightful size. Anything that passes through the arch is shrunk by magic. It's a perfect way to hide from our enemies, a single tree becomes as big as a city.'

'What a brilliant idea,' said Kit studying it. 'You could keep a whole country in a garden.'

Henry, still feeling woozy, wasn't so convinced. 'It's not that I mind being small,' he said. 'It's more that I'm worried about *them*—'

Following his gaze, Kit saw the ants, rank upon rank of them drawn up with the precision of soldiers on a military campaign. Each was fiery red, with thick brittle skin, a swollen body, an anvil shaped head and extraordinarily thin matchstick legs with feet like billhooks. By comparison they stood as large as wolves and were as strong as rhinoceroses. And, if this wasn't enough, the humming waves of fury coming off them were so powerful that they could be felt.

'They must think we're food or trespassers,' murmured Henry weakly. 'Either way it doesn't make it any better for us.'

The ants clicked their antennae like drumsticks; and one ant—a commanding general covered in scars—waved a log in the air like a mad caber tosser (although really it was the tiniest twig imaginable). And as they watched, the ant army increased rapidly, countless others pouring out from nest-holes, scrambling over each other in their eagerness to show their loyalty to the queen in the only way they knew how—by doing battle against her enemies.

Only Tita acted unconcerned.

'Don't worry about them,' she said lightly. 'The ants are our second line of defence after the gorgons.'

This was easy for her to say, but a hundred gigantic

advancing ants all thinking as if with one mind and all in a passion of fury, are not easily ignored. Kit was so busy watching their lines getting closer and closer that he was only vaguely aware of something dropping from the branches of Mountain Tree. Then, in less time than it takes to let out a terrified scream, three hairy, chocolate-brown spiders with banded legs and six gleaming eyes apiece, swung down on the ends of thick silk ropes like insect commandos.

The first had the easiest task: it grabbed Tita and hauled her up. Henry's and Kit's spiders had a far harder job because both boys put up a tremendous fight against the hairy giants, who seemed quite puzzled that they did. In the end it was no contest. Kit found his arms pinned to his sides with silk and, while being held close to the spider's body by two hairy legs, was lifted off his feet, up and up ever higher into the tree. And, if being ambushed and grabbed by a spider wasn't bad enough, being casually tossed aside like the empty, sucked-dry skin of a bluebottle was ten times worse.

Kit tumbled through the air—

'Whaaaaaaaa!'

—and struck a huge trampoline. Only here, where things were not as they should be, the trampoline turned out to be a web spun from special stickyless thread.

Kit bounced to a standstill, Henry beside him; Tita sitting at the web's edge, her feet dangling through it, much amused by their pale faces.

'Thinking back,' she said with an innocent shrug, 'I probably should have warned you about the spiders. But don't worry, they're such dears and as friendly as ponies once they get to recognize you.'

'I s'pose they wouldn't hurt a fly,' said Kit darkly, struggling out of his silken bonds.

'Oh no—they'd definitely kill you if you were a fly.'

She leapt up brightly, balancing on a thread like a tightrope walker. 'Now the choice is yours. Either we can reach the next level of the tree by climbing webs, or I can whistle for another set of spiders. They'd be more than glad to take us.'

Henry looked mournful. 'I think I'd rather do without the spiders if it's all the same to you,' he said.

Tita grinned. 'Please yourself, but I somehow guessed that would be your answer.'

Climbing spiders' webs when there is barely half an inch of you from head to toe, is not unlike climbing a ship's rigging—and hard work at that! The webs swayed and trembled over breathtaking drops; while spiders kept careful watch on them from their crevice homes—six eyes aglow in a row like headlamps—as if pitying the poor clumsy humans for having only four limbs and such an ungainly climbing style. Henry found it most off-putting.

'Haven't they anything better to do with their time?' he complained loudly. 'Why can't they go somewhere else and polish their fangs with those hairy legs of theirs instead of waving them in my face? If I knew anything about spiders I'd swear they were laughing at me.'

At long last they reached the branch they needed, one of the tree's great twisted limbs which stretched out levelly and which, judging by the amount of activity to be seen upon it, was one of the oak's main highways and not just for enchanters but crawling things of every type. There were caterpillars, ladybirds, slow moving snails (some with riders and some without), and flocks of squeaking woodlice (which appeared to be kept as pets by younger wizards and witches and were as common and numerous as cats and dogs might otherwise have been). Tiny flying creatures made the air hum; and fireflies cast light which, shaded downwards by the leaves, gave everything a mysterious green luminosity.

Henry and Kit simply stood and gaped at every new wonder as it came along.

'So, not quite the ordinary old tree you first thought it was, after all?' remarked Tita gently mocking them.

Kit shook his head, his eyes very wide. 'Far from ordinary,' he managed to gasp, watching an elderly witch dragging an earwig on a lead—rather like a poodle but with many more legs to cock.

Yet amongst the outlandish sights it did him good to see some plain, old-fashioned magic. A group of grubby urchins on brooms came whizzing out from behind a leaf the size of a ceiling. 'Tita! Tita!' they called on spotting her. Kit felt his magic leap up, he guessed that this was her gang, like his own gang back home in London.

A short conversation in their own language followed, Kit not understanding at all, but recognizing the playful way they addressed each other and the affectionate teasing laughter. Tita shrugged a lot and had a look about her which said 'Well, see if I care!' Laughing, her gang flew off—to drop acorns on to ants, Kit wouldn't have been at all surprised to discover, or some similar mischief.

'What's wrong?' Henry asked Tita.

'Nothing I can't deal with,' she said crossly. 'My mother . . . She's playing the Red Indian.'

Henry and Kit stared at her. Then Henry smiled. 'Oh, I see . . . *On the warpath*. Your mother is on the warpath after you.'

'That's what I said, didn't I?' snapped Tita. 'Come on. I best get this over with.'

She walked them along the branch towards the trunk, on the way stepping aside for spiders and colourful bugs of all shapes and sizes. In front of a hollow just where the branch and trunk joined, a witch stood waiting impatiently, in her hand a wand very nearly as tall as she was. She had wild hair streaked with lightning forks of

126

white and her black robes were cut zigzagged at the sleeves and hem and hung with tiny gold charms. She saw them a matter of seconds after they sighted her and came striding up angrily; and she was not alone. Her every step was accompanied by a host of birds—but birds the size of gnats, indicating they must have arrived at the tree through the magic arch. There were sparrows, parakeets, robins, hawks, crows . . . and these were only the ones Kit took in at a glance. A little higher soared a pair of fierce eagles; and by her ear, never moving more than a fraction away from it, hovered a humming bird more brightly coloured than a jewel in an Indian prince's turban.

'Uh-oh, trouble,' said Tita under her breath.

'Ti-ta!' bellowed her mother. 'Plague of my life, *where* have you been, child? I have been beside myself, at my wits' end, almost crazy with worry. And now you are here I don't know what to do first—beat you or hug you—perhaps I shall do both—you foolish, unthinking, disobedient girl!'

'Mother, it—'

'And look at you—look at you! There's hardly a clean patch left on you, and you've been using magic to cover up your bruises—don't deny it, I can tell.'

'Yes, but—'

'I told you not to take any unnecessary risks, but did you listen to me?'

'I tried—'

'Oh, there now, are you satisfied, I'm crying. Look—look tears! And if my magic lies stone dead inside me from endlessly fretting about you, it'll be you who's to blame . . . You . . . You . . . *Oh*—'

She set about Tita with her wand, giving her a couple of hefty wacks across her shoulders, which Tita took unflinchingly. Then she hugged her in an embrace which, if anything, appeared more likely to do her harm. She hit her again. She hugged her again. And every time her wand came down, little birds flew from her like sparks and pecked at Tita's hand; and when she was hugged they stroked her hair with their wings.

'Mama—Mama—I am here now,' said Tita growing quickly impatient of the hit-hug routine.

Her mother wiped away a tear and waved her arms, everything about her dramatic and wildly passionate.

'I see that. But you should have sent word, child. The last I heard you were being taken to the witch-hunt. I thought you dead. Why didn't you send a simple message or token to let me know you were safe?'

'Don't cry, Mama, please. A message couldn't come any quicker than we have and surely that is better in the end, isn't it? And look at me. I'm still standing aren't I? My English friends here rescued me from the hunt: I was scooped up on a flying-carpet, and we used the trees in the forest for our guides, and now we are here. It wasn't so terrible really.'

More calmly Tita's mother blinked across at Kit and Henry and smiled gratefully. A robin landing on Kit's shoulder gently nuzzled his ear.

The witch wiped her face on the back of her sleeve suddenly embarrassed. 'What must you think of me?' she said. 'I must look a fright . . . forgetting myself . . . firing off so. Tita, you should have stopped me! Let me introduce myself—Margha Stara, Tita's mother. So pleased to meet you. And you, you are all wet and cold. Hungry too I shouldn't wonder.'

'Well . . . yes,' said Henry, reminded that the apple he had eaten an hour ago was ancient history as far as his stomach was concerned.

'I thought as much. Come in, come in. There is always room for our friends by the fire.'

And with her arm around Tita's waist and a flock of

birds circling about her head, she led them up some pouting fungus steps into the hollow and the very heart of the tree. Here a small fire burned—rather recklessly in Kit's view—still, at first it was much too dark and shadowy for him to make out anything at all clearly. Slowly he grew aware of a couple of large spiders staring at him as if he were something caught in a web; then meat—like the side of an ox—cooking over the flames (roast vole if only he knew it); then dim figures seated around it. But he was totally unprepared for what he saw next.

Suddenly, as if a bomb had gone off in his face, he leapt back with a shout, startling Henry and setting all the birds whirling and cawing.

'Why is he here?' shouted Kit pointing angrily at a figure by the fire's edge.

'Kit—what's wrong?' asked Henry. Then he too saw. 'Oh . . . Mr Skinner,' he said weakly.

Unchanged from the hunt, his buttons undone and mud caked thickly to the soles of his boots, Mr Skinner stood up and awkwardly removed his bowler hat.

'Ah, Kit: good evening, Prince,' he said softly 'I was wondering when you'd arrive.'


The atmosphere became very tense; enchanter elders turned to each other, not knowing why precisely but feeling it like a chill in the air. Margha Stara felt it too; she stooped over the fire to sprinkle a special powder onto the flames, turning the harsh reds and oranges to softer blues and purples. The flames no longer flickered but flowed upwards so slowly that it was possible to follow the life of a single flame in every detail; and here-and-gone sparks mellowed into lazy gleams, as when sunlight is caught in the dimple of a sluggish river. The reason she did this was to bring calm, especially to Kit who stood in the darkest corner, arms folded and mouth drawn tight, preferring the company of monstrous spiders to that of Mr Skinner.

Henry tried his best to smooth matters, but Kit's mood was particularly black; his magic simmered dangerously inside him.

'Come on, Kit,' whispered his friend. 'There must be a good reason for Mr Skinner being here. After all, the enchanters wouldn't be so foolish as to invite him in and act so friendly towards him if there wasn't.'

'Oh, he's a sharp one,' said Kit bitterly, and not bothering to lower his voice or caring who heard. 'He must have tricked his way into Mountain Tree; but jus' you wait, Henry, he will betray every last one of us. He'll do it when the moment suits him best.'

'Look, Margha Stara is giving him some food and Tita is taking him a mug of beer—they don't seem at all concerned.'

Kit scowled even more. 'For a magic-hater he has somehow managed to bewitch the whole lot of 'em. Only I know all about him and what he is like—really like—so he better not try to bewitch me or then he'll find out whose magic is stronger.'

'Well, can't we at least hear what he has to say before we decide on anything?' The smell of cooking meat wafted over temptingly, too temptingly for Henry. 'And perhaps we could get something to eat too, it'll make you feel better once you have food inside you.'

Kit glared at him in disbelief. 'Eat? Henry, you don't understand do you? How can I possibly sit down with that magic-hater and eat? The tiniest mouthful will choke me.' He glanced across at the fire. Tita paused and smiled at him uncertainly.

'Huh!' said Kit turning away. 'I don't know how Tita can calmly just hand that man bread that isn't poisoned or full of worms. Has she forgotten that a few hours ago he was hunting her down like a frightened rabbit?'

'That's what I'm saying. Let's go and hear how Mr Skinner explains himself,' repeated Henry patiently.

With great reluctance Kit allowed himself to be led back to the fire. Old wizards and witches looked up at him, smiling, their wrinkled faces moonlight blue in the steady glow of the flames. One or two muttered a *Well Wish* as a greeting and Kit felt them break against his skin, fresh and tingling.

He sat down heavily on a shrew's skull, as far away from Mr Skinner as possible. Margha Stara brought him some food on a leaf and thrust it at him with the instruction 'Eat'; but pointedly he set it down at his feet, his appetite not in keeping with his hunger. Through flames that waved in slow dancing ribbons like river weed, he concentrated every bit of his hostile stare on the detective upon the opposite side.

'Deny it was you in the photograph I saw at Professor Muir's house,' he began angrily. 'Tell me again it wasn't you with all your magic-hating friends!'

Mr Skinner gazed across at him without showing a flicker of emotion. 'It was me,' he said quietly. And as Kit sat back in triumph he went on, 'But as usual, Kit, you read the situation completely wrong. They are not and never were my friends—no . . . You see my real job at Scotland Yard is with the Department of Magical Crimes, working *against* magic-haters.'

Kit gave a dismissive snort. 'Never heard of it.'

'I didn't expect you to, it is highly secret and with good reason: we deal with dangerous men with dangerous ideas; we have to keep a close eye on them and their business. The best way of doing this, I have found, is to pretend to be one of them and join their ranks. It was unfortunate that I happened to be photographed wearing those ridiculous robes, and the photograph was published in the newspaper.'

Kit was unconvinced. 'But you never did like me because of what I am—a wizard. Every time I used my magic I felt your anger and *that* was real.'

'Of course,' replied Mr Skinner. 'You weren't to know but you were drawing unwanted attention to yourself— and to me. You might have spoilt everything. It is the way of how things go that I need to win over the trust of the enemy first. They would be watching me all the while, reporting back to the people who matter. It did me no favours at all to be seen in the company of a—if you'll forgive me here—showy little wizard.'

'*Hmph*. What about when you betrayed me . . . and . . . and when you joined the witch-hunt against Tita?'

'If by betrayed you mean the time you rode a broom back into the palace and I met you on the wall, you were spotted and reported to the Magic Watch by at least a dozen people. And before you ask, I was signalling to some of my friends here—real enchanters' (Tita nodded her head in agreement) 'forced to enter the city and encounter its dangers because my wireless was *mysteriously* broken.'

Kit looked away.

'And then it was fortunate for you that Tita was following you through the palace this morning and allowed herself to be taken by the Sniffer in your place. Yes, I did join the hunt against her, I felt I was being tested by those who hate magic, and couldn't very well refuse; but my real intention was to help Tita. I was going to break away from the others, cut her hands free, and give her my horse so she could gallop away to safety. It would then be a matter of telling my companions that my horse had thrown me to the ground and hoping they believed me. Tita took a great risk, and as it was events did not turn

132

out as planned: I got caught up in a tree and for a while things started to look grim. Thankfully you arrived on your flying-carpet and the rest you know better than me.'

A pair of wrens flew over to Tita and nestled themselves under her chin. 'Ah, Mama, I'm fine now. Really. Hardly a scratch left on me,' she protested blandly.

Kit slowly reached down, picked up a hunk of bread and bit it thoughtfully. 'But that still doesn't explain the warning left for me on the day I arrived. You told Tita to do something with my bag and the next time I saw it all my wizard gowns were torn to shreds and smeared in blood.'

'I told Tita to go through your bag and remove anything connected with magic. I was concerned. What if a prying servant had gone through it later and realized the truth? If word had got out that you were a wizard, well . . . you've met the Magic Watch for yourself.'

'But the blood—'

Here Tita had something to say.

'When I opened your bag,' she said, 'I found a nasty surprise waiting inside—a creature like nothing I had ever come across before, not even in the forest. It was in such a temper, which it had already taken out on everything in your bag, that there was nothing left to sort through but tatters. When the creature saw me it leapt up and took me completely by surprise. I wasn't expecting it. And its teeth were as sharp as needles. That was *my* blood you saw, Kit, my hand still has the scars.'

Kit gave a nervous laugh. 'Luddite!' he cried. 'I wondered how he got here. He must have been hiding in my bag all the while . . . I suppose that's another piece of the jigsaw fitted into place.'

Idly he picked at the crust on his bread. 'Mr Skinner . . . ' he began hesitantly. 'I reckon I owe you an apology—prob'ly the biggest I've ever made in my whole life. I'm sorry for everything I've ever done against you—breaking your wireless and all them other things . . . I feel pretty stupid now if you want to know.'

'Good—so you deserve to,' said Mr Skinner, although smiling and sounding good natured.

Henry, who had been listening intently to everything discussed, leaned a little more forward. 'Mr Skinner,' he said. 'Perhaps you can explain one more thing to me.'

'I'd be happy to, Prince, if I can.'

'Now I see that being my bodyguard was more or less a pretence, what is your real reason for coming to Callalabasa?'

'Ah . . . my real reason.' The detective smiled grimly. 'For some time now Scotland Yard has been receiving reports from our agents such as Margha Stara and Tita here of a mechanical monster being secretly built in Callalabasa, a war machine so different it will make every army in the world useless at a stroke. No pictures of it exist, but from the little we know I can tell you this: it is crewless, controls itself, and is protected by the toughest armour ever made, so is very nearly indestructible. It also possesses terrifying fire-power and is able to destroy whatever stands in its path; but the most frightening thing of all is that once it is started it cannot be stopped, because there is no possible way of getting inside to reach the controls. We have found out next to nothing about who is behind it but we do know one thing for certain—the machine's name. It's called the Scarab.'

'The Scarab,' repeated Kit. He wrinkled up his nose. 'That's a horrible ugly sounding name, but from what you say it deserves it.'

Henry nodded in agreement. 'Callalabasa seems a strange out-of-the-way place to be doing all this, don't you think, Mr Skinner?'

'Not at all,' answered Mr Skinner. 'Callalabasa is

134

perfect. We believe the maker of the Scarab wishes to show off the machine and all it can do by means of a war. Then, when the world sees exactly what the machine is capable of, every country big or small will clamour to own as many as it can afford—either to crush its enemies or to prevent itself from being crushed. Such a demand will make the Scarab's creator fabulously wealthy. I dread to say it but Callalabasa is where this handy little war is due to take place—a war against the enchanters. This is the reason the magic-haters are involved, and why false enchanters have been busily stirring up the people against magic. Despite this the magic-haters are merely servants in this affair, serving an as yet unknown master.'

As shocking as this idea was, Kit did not believe it would happen. 'How can a war take place while the enchanters have Mountain Tree to escape to?' he said.

'Ah, but do we?' said Margha Stara gloomily. 'We believe our enemies already know it exists.'

'How?' demanded Kit.

Margha Stara stroked a small sleepy owl that sat in her lap. 'All enchanters who come to Mountain Tree are taught to bewitch themselves with a special charm of forgetting,' she explained. 'So if they ever leave and fall into the Watch's hands they won't be able to tell them a word about our hideaway. But then about two or three months ago an old gypsy witch called Pampla Droiga was captured. She bewitched herself and was sure the secret was safe, but our spies in the city—' (She smiled absently at the little owl who was probably one of them.) '—our spies informed us that the Watch used the services of an old vampire called Count Drohlomski against her. The disgusting creature is an expert hypnotizer and knows how to crack open the pathways of the mind. We believe he found out about Mountain Tree in return for a small reward or some privilege or other. As for Pampla Droiga, she was found wandering the forest completely out of her wits. Destroyed by the vampire.'

'I can believe every bad word I hear about Count Drohlomski,' said Kit shuddering. 'I met him through sheer bad luck and only just managed to escape myself.'

'And things have happened since,' continued Margha Stara. 'Strangers have been seen in the forest close to the waterfall; and once an airship hovered right over the tree for about twenty minutes. We saw men with telescopes peering down. If they know where we are they can drive us out into the path of their terrible machine any time they please.'

'Where is the machine?' asked Henry.

Mr Skinner sighed and stared dejectedly into the slow blue flames. 'I don't know,' he admitted. 'I hoped to find out through my contacts with the magic-haters, but so far I haven't been able to win over their complete trust; and time is running out, the machine must be nearly ready. If it isn't found soon Callalabasa will be torn apart, and the war once it starts is unstoppable.'

Very quietly, almost as if surprised to hear himself speak, Kit said, 'Mr Skinner . . . I think *I* know where you can find what you are looking for.'

# Chapter Twelve

K it quickly told them what he had seen on the night he had followed the pretend enchanters, and how they had disappeared almost before his eyes, down a dead-end alley. For some reason his heart bumped excitedly and he could hardly catch his breath. Mr Skinner made him tell everything again, only more slowly; and yet a third time, this time jotting down details in a notebook with a stub of pencil, quite looking and sounding the man from Scotland Yard. Did Kit know the name of the alley? No. Could he find it again. Yes . . . he thought so. 'Are you positive about that?' asked Mr Skinner gravely.

'Positive,' answered Kit with a firm nod.

Mr Skinner asked many more questions, some that made Kit exasperated wondering what on earth they had to do with the secret entrance.

Then abruptly Mr Skinner snapped shut his book and slipped it back into his pocket. 'Thank you, Kit, that is all,' he said.

'What happens now?' asked Henry.

'Lots,' replied Mr Skinner. 'But only if you are prepared to help me. It's best to act quickly—tonight if possible. I want to see for myself what Kit has discovered and whether or not it really is the Scarab's secret hiding place. Well, Kit, do you feel you can trust me enough to take me to Luca on that flying-carpet of yours?'

'You bet!—that is, if you're willing to risk your neck riding the skies with me.'

'Oh, I'll risk it,' smiled Mr Skinner.

'And our witches and wizards will do their bit too,' said Margha Stara. 'I will send birds to every enchanter in the forest telling them to meet up at Mountain Tree. If we fly with you we can spin a dense fog to hide your approach; and should anything go wrong we will be close at hand with our magic. For too long we have sat back and done nothing hoping that everything will work out right by itself. It hasn't. If it comes to a fight we shall be ready.'

'Good,' said Mr Skinner. 'In the meantime I suggest we grab a few hours shut-eye—it has been an eventful day so far and it looks very much set to continue that way.'

'Couldn't agree more,' said Henry stretching. 'I think this has been the longest day of my life.'

Kit and Henry had the impression they were welcome to stay in the hollow as Mr Skinner did—lying down by the blue fire, a cobweb blanket pulled up over him—if it wasn't for Tita having other ideas. She led the short climb up to the next branch—to an abandoned bird's nest built in a fork in the twigs and completely hidden by leaves. The nest was warm, dry, and cosily lined with downy feathers and fresh, scented moss. And without the need to be told, Henry and Kit both slid down from the sides and snuggled themselves under; and if Henry was asleep first, Kit was a very close second.

At different times in the past, Kit had been awoken by a kitten leaping upon his quilt and by a friendly dog licking his face, but he didn't think he could ever—*ever*—get used to being woken up by a spider! It came as too great a shock, and gave him the unnerving feeling that instead of being properly awake he had merely slipped into a different dream. As it was he jumped up in alarm before remembering that giant spiders were all perfectly normal;

138

then his breath came out of him in one long thankful gasp.

A neat silvery-grey spider with bristles over its fangs like a moustache and, more endearingly, a clump of hair that stood on end on its head, watched him, amused. It waved its legs and Kit realized it was pointing. Turning his head slightly, he saw a second, much bigger spider, trying to remain upright as Carpet (roped to its back) struggled to break free. Having been awoken by Kit's shout of surprise, Henry took out his penknife and cut the silken threads; and the big spider scuttled away with the silvery-grey little one, much relieved to be rid of such an ungrateful, bad-tempered burden.

Carpet gave Kit a terrific hug.

Kit laughed, but then remembering Tita's warning, glanced up through the leaves for moths. He saw it was still dark; Henry couldn't stop yawning. Then Tita appeared on her broom, flitting above the nest like a mosquito.

'Hurry up,' she called down, 'Mr Skinner is getting impatient. Here, I brought you cloaks for the journey.'

She threw them down and they put them on, grateful to have something to wear against the cold night. Then Tita flew with them to the hollow; she kept to the air while Carpet landed. Mr Skinner did indeed look impatient, climbing aboard without a word, his boots very muddy. Carpet gave a twitch of annoyance.

'Rise!' ordered Kit before it tried to throw him off, muddy boots and all.

Carpet rose bulging under the extra weight and followed Tita out of the tree. Then as if from nowhere they were suddenly joined by hundreds of broomstick-riding witches and wizards, resembling in number and flight a squadron of swarming bees; and if this was so, Margha Stara was their queen, her birds streaming behind her like the tail of a comet.

She laughed recklessly. 'Was there ever a better night to be an enchanter?' she cried; and Kit, thrilled, felt his magic respond inside him.

Without a word of command the flying army swooped in from all directions to form a single line behind her, and passed one by one under the stone arch and through the parted waterfall; and once again their rightful size went streaking at full magic over the tops of the forest trees.

They flew high and fast through thin cold air, yet it wasn't long before Margha Stara fell back alongside Carpet. 'Land here,' she called to Kit, falling away at once in a stunningly fearless nosedive.

Together they put down at an old ruined abbey about a mile from the city. Fortunately the place had a reputation for being haunted so local people stayed well clear of it, especially at night.

The church building was open to the stars and its stone pillars were chopped off at various heights. The throng of enchanters crowded in (snapping their fingers at the ghosts who did dare to appear), filling the roofless space; their excitement raising little unexpected crackles and brief blue flames that flickered overhead like will-o'-the-wisps.

Margha Stara was helped up onto a pile of rubble and everyone fell silent to hear what she had to say. Speaking in her own language she told the gathering that the time had come to be brave and level headed, to be proud to be an enchanter, and to use their magic wisely in a worthwhile cause. Then when her fiery words had been roundly cheered, she gave precise instructions concerning the fog spell, which needed to be agreed upon so no one's magic reacted against anyone else's; after that was settled there came the matter of how best to cast it. At some risk to their own lives, it was decided they would fly around the city limits and weave the spell in midflight. Then when finally cast, Carpet could carry its passengers over the wall and the search for the Scarab's secret hideaway could begin.

Tita nudged Kit. 'Don't worry, I shall be right beside you,' she said. 'Just pray that Mama doesn't notice I'm missing when they go to fly off.'

There seemed precious little chance of that—Margha Stara was far too preoccupied just then with her flock of birds; Kit noticing that the shy seed eaters and waders had been mostly replaced by fierce looking eagles, hawks, ospreys, owls, and ravens. Margha Stara commanded with the power of a general, but this did not prevent fights in the ranks, with birds screeching at each other or making threatening pecking motions or slashing at the air with their talons. Of the smaller birds, only the jewelled hummingbird remained and that kept close to the witch's ear for fear of losing its life.

The signal to leave came when the birds took to the air in a teeming flock; Margha Stara followed, her hair falling wildly around her; and in groups or singly the other wizards and witches lifted from the ground like feathery snowflakes caught on a breeze.

'Give us twenty minutes to work our magic,' came Margha Stara's voice from somewhere in the lively skies above.

Mr Skinner pulled out his watch and nodded. When he looked up again a moment later the flying army had gone.

'It's going to seem a long wait,' said Henry.

'Needn't be,' said Kit remembering his weather control lessons back at Eton. 'Fog's a simple piece of magic, it should be thickening nicely in half the time.'

'*Twenty minutes*,' said Mr Skinner in a tone not to be argued with. He leaned his watch on a mossy stone so they could see for themselves the time pass by—

*Or not.* For although the luminous green second hand

141

swept busily around the numbers, the minute hand steadfastly refused to join the chase. If time wasn't exactly standing still it seemed to be going a good deal more slowly than it ought.

'Come on—come on,' urged Kit impatiently, half tempted to give the watch a helping nudge with his magic.

Infuriatingly Mr Skinner would not budge a single step until twenty minutes—and twenty minutes exactly—were shown to be up.

'Have patience,' he told Kit. 'You'll never make a good detective otherwise.'

'And you'll never make a wizard—nothin'll ever get done,' muttered Kit under his breath.

At long last Mr Skinner pocketed his watch; the riders quickly took up their places on Carpet and Tita summoned her broom. They rose levelly into the sky and Tita pointed.

'See—they've done it,' she cried.

They all turned towards Luca.

'My, how very strange,' said Henry.

Kit and the others had to agree. On such a beautiful clear cloudless night as this, with velvety starlight and excellent views for miles around, the thick wall of fog billowed oddly on the plain; and the flying figures before it spinning their spell appeared no more than insects.

Speeding towards it, the shifting wall of fog grew and grew until it towered above them. Seeing them come, the other witches and wizards reined up their brooms to let them pass, some calling out 'Good luck'. Mr Skinner gravely raised his bowler to them like the Prince of Wales at Ascot, while Tita fell in close beside Carpet to escape her mother's watchful eye.

The fog struck cold the instant they pierced it; Kit shivered and pulled up the hood of his cloak. They crossed the wall unseen and below them made out vague roofs and chimneys but nothing in the way of a reliable landmark.

'We have to land,' said Kit. 'I won't be able to recognize anything from this height.'

Mr Skinner nodded reluctantly. 'Only if you're sure we're in the right part of the city,' he said.

'We should be,' answered Kit not sounding as convinced as he would have liked.

Nearer the ground the fog lay even thicker so that Kit struggled to see, and he began to worry that now they were inside Luca the fog might be more of a hindrance than a help. They landed on wet cobbles and through shreds of drifting mist Kit made out the dark outlines of tall shuttered buildings. Then he turned and saw a fountain, a double-headed bear dribbling water. It gave him a jolt. Unless there were two such fountains in the city he now knew exactly where they were. He felt his worries lift off him like a weight.

He glanced about to see if their arrival had gone unnoticed and when quite sure it had he swiftly rolled up Carpet and tucked it under his cloak (Tita hiding her broom similarly). 'This way, everyone,' he whispered. 'Don't lose sight of me.'

He strode ahead with confidence; Mr Skinner came next, and Tita and Henry behind him. Mist coiled around them in the narrow deserted alleys, and through it painted eyes had an unnerving habit of looming out when least expected. One particularly piercing eye made Henry jump and he struck Mr Skinner in the back.

'Why have we stopped?' he whispered over the detective's shoulder.

'Because we are here,' replied Kit. 'The dead-end alley where I saw the pretend enchanters do their disappearing act.'

'You're sure?' said Mr Skinner looking about. 'This is definitely the place?'

Kit nodded. 'See, that's my mark on the wall over there, no doubt about it.'

Four pairs of narrowed eyes peered into the blind alley. As before three solid walls created the sides and end. Not a single window. Not a single door. Mr Skinner now saw it fell to him to make the next move . . . Casually—his eyes darting from side to side beneath the brim of his hat—he walked in, each step tapped out in the darkness.

More nervously Henry, Kit, and Tita crept after him, to the furthest end where the detective had already made an interesting discovery.

'Just as I thought,' he said without glancing back. 'Doors painted to look like solid brick.'

'Is there a handle or some means to open them?' asked Henry.

'Not that I can see—' Mr Skinner stamped down his foot. 'Wait, the floor,' he said, 'that's wooden too. At a guess I'd say that the whole system is balanced similar to a weighbridge, which means that the doors should open automatically with the right amount of weight pressing down—say, a couple of horses and their riders. This would solve the mystery of how the band Kit saw was able to vanish so quickly.'

'So our weight alone isn't enough?' said Tita.

Mr Skinner shook his head.

'All right, let's get summat heavy that will make it enough,' yelped Kit rushing off. He returned a moment later hauling a full dustbin. 'There's plenty more round the corner,' he panted at the others.

Henry looked shocked. 'Aren't they smelly?' he asked.

'Yes—very. Now for goodness' sake forget you're a prince, Henry, and go and fetch one.'

Tita and Henry dashed around the corner and returned

as quickly as Kit had, similarly carrying a dustbin each; and as soon as they stepped upon the wooden floor their combined weight made something happen as Mr Skinner guessed it would. The floor sank by several inches and the doors began to move. All eyes were firmly fixed to the dark opening as it widened slowly in front of them. Yet for all the heart-stoppingness of the moment, nothing could be seen, not even now, with both doors fully apart.

Kit turned to Mr Skinner. 'Do we go on?' he whispered.

'If we hope to find the Scarab, we must.' And he went forward past the doors.

Then, because his weight no longer helped to keep them open, the doors started to close, forcing Kit and his friends to leap smartly through the narrowing gap before it disappeared altogether and they were left stranded outside.

The heavy doors bumped shut, the sound giving the impression that they were in a sizeable space, but it was dark—darker than a troll's lair—making it quite impossible to see. Kit pointed and a pale quaking imitation of one of his usual glow-balls drifted off the tip of his finger, taking several moments to settle; when it did, the darkness was pushed back as if by the flame of a pauper's candle.

'Hey, look at this,' whispered Tita crossing to a row of black robes hanging on hooks. Next to them were pairs of little red light-bulbs wired up to battery packs, clearly meant to be worn on belts concealed beneath the same loose-fitting gowns.

'The glowing red eyes, I suppose,' she said, picking up a set and tossing them aside in disgust.

Henry had made an even more startling find—a kind of shooting gallery not unlike those set up in booths at fairgrounds, but this one had a selection of real—bullet firing—guns. Thirty paces away the targets were pumpkins with faces painted on them, some half blasted away.

Crossing over, Henry lifted one of the undamaged pumpkins from the shelf and frowned.

'This looks like it might be King Eugen,' he said.

'It is,' said Tita. 'There's its paper crown on the floor.'

Mr Skinner was not a bit surprised.

'The coronation is a matter of hours away,' he said. 'And a war, like a fire, needs a good spark to get it going. What better way than killing the new king and laying the blame at the door of enchanters? These are ruthless people who will use whatever means they can . . . Where's Kit?'

Henry looked up aware that Kit was no longer with them; he turned sensing something wrong.

'What is it, Kit? You've gone as white as a sheet.'

They all stared at him.

Wordlessly Kit undid his top button and pulled out the half-forgotten charm he'd promised his father to wear at all times.

Its warning glowed sharply.

'*Stafford Sparks*,' he gasped. 'He's here! It's him behind the Scarab—it has been all along.'

And just as he said this they became aware of voices in the room next door.

# Chapter Thirteen

K it's magic churned inside him; knowing his old enemy was so close had come as a total shock . . . and yet, thinking about it more calmly, was it *so* surprising after all? Sparks must have timed his prison escape to coincide with the Scarab's completion; while most probably the terrible machine had been planned long ago when Sparks was still Superintendent of Scientific Progress at the Temple of Science—a favourite of the Queen and more or less free to do what he wished . . .

Kit must have been frowning as he thought. He saw Henry gaze worriedly at him. He thrust away the charm and hastily did up his buttons. 'I'm fine,' he whispered. From the corner of his eye he caught Mr Skinner take a revolver off the shelf, weigh it in his hand a moment, and slip it into his pocket. Kit took a stiff breath to steady his magic so as to be ready for trouble too.

'Mr Skinner,' said Tita looking thoughtful herself. 'What does the Scarab actually look like? I mean, how will we know when we find it?'

The detective filled his other pocket with bullets. 'Don't you worry, Tita, you'll not mistake it for anything else.'

He crossed to the door and put his ear to it. The voices on the other side sounded muffled and distant. He turned back to Tita and Kit. 'Listen, I desperately need a good sighting of that machine,' he said. 'The more we find out about it the better prepared we'll be.'

Tita nodded realizing what he was asking. 'How about

we go on a short mind-walk for you,' she offered. 'It'll only take a moment and will tell us roughly how things are. You with me on this, Kit?'

'Right on your heels,' he said. 'But take care not to brush against anyone. One little touch and Sparks'll guess that we're on to his game.'

With their eyes shut tightly they sent out their minds—under the door and into the unknown of the next room, fluttering and cautiously feeling their way. There they clung to the wall like mussels to a rock—as Kit had said, they didn't want to betray their presence by thoughtlessly drifting into one of the enemy, that would be tragic. Around them the air was still, undisturbed by movement or the breath of speakers. Lifting, they floated back to the empty bodies that waited for them.

'Nothin' this end,' reported Kit. 'Even so, it doesn't mean eyes aren't looking in the direction of the door and spot it the second it opens.'

'Frankly that's a risk I'm willing to take,' said Mr Skinner gravely.

He reached out for the door handle. Kit and the others watched in silence, each wondering how something so simple and everyday as opening a door could suddenly be turned into a kind of slow torture. Soundlessly the handle went down. Yet the suspense only increased as the door started to open inch by inch until there was just enough room for Mr Skinner to squeeze his head through.

He took a long look then beckoned them to join him. One after another their heads moved around the door, anxious to see.

Behind it lay a large well equipped engineer's workshop, dimly lit: a few naked light bulbs hanging down on wires. Around the walls were benches and well ordered tool shelves; oil patches stained the concrete floor. But these were little more than details: of far greater importance to them was the large object that dominated the centre of the room—yet disappointingly was concealed beneath a white dust sheet right down to the ground.

Mr Skinner cursed sharply under his breath—to come so far and then be denied a single glimpse . . .

Henry kept wriggling.

'F'goodness' sake, Henry, keep your head still,' hissed Kit.

'I can't help it, I'm trying to find Sparks,' said Henry defensively. 'Where is he? Do you think he may have already gone?'

Kit lifted his head to sniff the air. As distinctive as a polecat's stench was the smell of Stafford Sparks's cigars: Kit remembered reading about them in many of the newspapers at the time of Sparks's trial. They were handmade on the best tobacco plantation in all of Cuba— from the best leaves grown in the best corner of the best field, which had just the right amount of rain and the most perfect ripening sunlight; each finished cigar cost as much as a working man's weekly wage, and they went by the name of Pope Honeydew's fingers. They caused a stir at the trial because the judge who heard it was a well known miser who lived on bread and cheese, by the light of one candle, and mended holes in his shoes with cardboard. He was as much outraged by this show of extravagance as he was by Sparks's robbing the Bank of England, and it probably accounted for another three years on his sentence.

Then Kit peered a little harder.

'No—look over there,' he whispered; and they saw a tell-tale plume of cigar smoke rising from the far side of the sheeted Scarab.

Then Sparks spoke and it gave them a thorough jolt to hear his voice so close and clear.

'Tighten it by another three degrees, and I'll hold you

personally responsible if it's done another screw-thread more,' he said harshly, speaking to one of his engineers.

'Yes, sir, Mr Sparks, at once, sir,' said the engineer slavishly obedient.

For a while after no more was heard but the sound of someone fine tuning part of the machine. Kit was getting a stiff neck. As he was about to suggest they slip away quietly while they still had the chance, a bell sounded and Stafford Sparks passed into sight crossing to answer a speaking-tube.

Kit's eyes latched on to him in the same fascinated way they would to a ghost. It amounted to the same thing. If ever there was a person he never thought to see again in this life it was Stafford Sparks. But there he was very much flesh and blood, and exactly how Kit remembered— impressively tall, thin, and commanding, with a thick moustache and mutton-chop whiskers, yet without so much as a single white hair to show for all the time he had been locked away in Wormwood Scrubs. Confidently he sucked on one of his scandalously expensive cigars, the little silver spanner he wore for good luck twinkling on his neck-tie. In such dreary surroundings he proved to be remarkably well dressed, his top hat shiny and new; and altogether he had the air about him of a duke on his way to his club.

'Umm? Yes . . . Come up straight away. I'm opening the door now,' he said into the tube. He hung it up and pulled a lever to unlock a door.

'This promises to be interesting,' murmured Mr Skinner. 'I shall be pleased to have the names of all his cronies.'

A door on the opposite side opened (there must be at least two outer doors, thought Kit) and a group of men entered out of the night; amongst them were faces instantly recognizable. First came Captain Slobbahn of the

150

Magic Watch surrounded by a number of his officers, and behind them Señor Pufni flashed his dark eyes dramatically. Far more unexpected, however, in such a parcel of rogues, was the king's uncle, Duke Liechenspit. But then, as Tita pointed out, he did stand to gain the crown if ever Eugen were done away with.

He stepped forward shaking the damp off his coat.

'Dear Mr Sparks,' he said, 'do forgive us for keeping you waiting, but what a night—what a witch's brew it is out there.'

'*What?*' Sparks's expression twisted.

Duke Liechenspit realized he had made an unfortunate error. 'Forgive me, it is a saying here in this rural backwater. In dear old England you would have the sense to describe it as a *pea-souper.*' And he smiled smoothly.

Kit, busily watching the two men, felt a sharp dig in his side. 'Kit, I'm worried about the Sniffer,' said Tita. 'What if he catches a whiff of our magic?'

Kit immediately saw the danger—he had completely forgotten Señor Pufni and his dubious gift. Even now Señor Pufni was raising his head, the sprouts from both nostrils trembling like diviner's twigs . . . sensing something both familiar and less pleasant to him beneath the rich sweet smell of Mr Sparks's cigar.

Then the perfect solution presented itself. Oily and anxious to please, Captain Slobbahn took out a little silver box beautifully shaped like a skull (and no doubt stolen, like so much he owned) and began to offer around a pinch of snuff to each of the company.

'Señor?'

The Sniffer glowered down with disdain at the snuff box held out to him. 'I do not partake,' he boomed loftily. 'I hold my nose in the highest esteem, it is like a sacred temple—my sense of smell a gift from the gods.'

Kit pointed.

Captain Slobbahn's arm jerked, throwing the entire contents of the snuff box straight into the Sniffer's face. He let out a roar of outrage then started to sneeze with surprising violence. Kit thought he might explode; while Captain Slobbahn was left foolishly stammering apologies. 'I'm sorry, señor, I don't know how it happened . . . '

'Good shot,' chuckled Henry.

A bad tempered argument broke out before them, Señor Pufni's eyes streaming; and every time he sneezed his handkerchief filled out like a sail-cloth in a gale. Captain Slobbahn shouted at his men, convinced one of them had shoved him, but each one hotly protested his innocence while accusing the person next to him. Finally Sparks could stand it no longer. He struck a metal plate with a hammer until it silenced them all.

'Gentlemen—gentlemen, may I remind you that we are here tonight for one reason and one reason only. And, in case anyone has forgotten, let me refresh his memory in the best possible way.'

With that he marched over to a corner of the dust sheet and tugged. The sheet slid away into folds upon the floor . . . and after so much guesswork and imagining, the Scarab was finally revealed.

And what a brute it was. Kit stared at it hardly daring to blink, the machine had such truly menacing presence. In shape it resembled nothing so much as a gigantic stag beetle, with spiked mandibles capable of seizing and puncturing a steam-wagon. It was black and lustreless; its antennae were two extended rifle barrels and down its spine and around its body were cannon covering every point of approach. Twin smoke stacks rose behind its head and it possessed six jointed legs to sweep every obstacle from its path and protect the eight pairs of wheels that in time would give it motion. Built of hard plate and rivet, the Scarab was nothing but a sinister machine of death and its looks reflected that perfectly.

Recovering from his initial shock, Mr Skinner took out his notebook and made a rapid sketch.

'Simply breathtaking,' purred the duke, drifting across and stroking an iron flank as though petting a living creature—perhaps one born in prehistoric times with volcanoes erupting and sulphurous swamps bubbling. 'When I am king, Mr Sparks, my first duty will be to raise a statue in your honour. *To Stafford Sparks, a genius of science* I will have carved on its base and fresh flowers—lilies, I think—shall be laid before it every week.'

'Jumping the gun somewhat, Duke,' remarked Sparks drily. 'Before you can go putting up statues to me or anyone else, you first have to make yourself king. Is that matter in hand?'

'Oh that,' said the duke as if nothing important. 'My men are positioned inside the palace. They have their enchanter disguises, they will not fail me. Tomorrow in the cathedral as those gathered to watch raise their voices to cry "Long live the King!", a single shot will ring out and make sure my idiot nephew's life is a good deal shorter than most there could imagine.' He smiled that creepy smile of his. 'Naturally afterwards I shall play the grief struck uncle perfectly and shed endless tears for the young fool. But then, as new king, I shall grow firm and strong I shall demand war and vengeance on those evil enchanters who have robbed us of our darling little Eugen. Airships will be summoned to drive them out of their forest hideout and provoke them into attacking Luca. After that, Mr Sparks, I believe the show is yours, yours and the beautiful Scarab here.'

Their uncaring laughter made Mr Skinner angry. He put away his notebook. 'Come on, I've heard about enough of this sickening rubbish,' he said.

They all had and were glad to back away unseen. But as they hurried past the shooting gallery (where the duke's assassin had perfected tomorrow's deadly shot) they saw to their horror the outer doors slowly begin to move apart—and it wasn't because of anything they had done to make them open either!

Outside in the alley three hooded riders sat on three dark mares. The riders' piercing red eyes fixed Kit and his friends in their spindly beams; and knowing them to be fake made them no less scary.

'Pretend enchanters!' uttered Henry.

Tita cast down her broom. She pointed and shot a flare amongst them, setting the horses rearing. Henry glanced worriedly behind. He knew it was asking too much for the shouts and terrified whinnies to pass unheard by Sparks and the other plotters.

Sure enough, seconds later, the workshop door flew open and Captain Slobbahn appeared at the head of his men, pistol unholstered. Kit's simmering magic was more than ready. Taking great delight he bowled a ball of spinning flame, and the Magic Watch fell aside like skittles—the captain's howl loudest of all as the door slammed shut.

'We shan't see them again in a hurry,' said Kit, dusting his hands in satisfaction.

He was right; inside the workshop was disarray.

'We're found out!' wailed the captain of the secret police. He staggered in confusion, magic still ringing in his ears. 'Wizards—twenty of them at least, maybe more.'

Señor Pufni let out a terrific bellow. 'I knew I smelt something foul—foul and rotten like a week old corpse on the end of a gibbet!'

'This should not be happening,' lamented Duke Liechenspit. 'We have lost control. We have lost everything . . .'

Amongst the storm of raised voices, Stafford Sparks's voice was the only one to remain calm and controlled.

'Can't you see—this couldn't have come at a more convenient moment,' he said. 'Gentlemen, kindly make an orderly exit, I believe the war has been declared for us—so naturally we must protect ourselves with every means available. Come—come, Duke, don't look so downhearted, the king's life may yet be lost in the confusion of battle. You may get to wear your pretty gold crown. Hurry along, gentlemen, I will follow directly I have fired up the Scarab . . . Then we can see exactly how feeble their magic really is, come twenty wizards or twenty-thousand of the devils.'

# Chapter Fourteen

Despite their outwardly fearsome appearance the pretend enchanters fled at the first sign of trouble, leaving Tita and Kit struggling with their magic to keep open the heavy outer doors in case they needed a speedy escape. Knowing that time was short, Mr Skinner and Henry crept back to the closed workshop door.

They listened there intently, Mr Skinner gripping the revolver. No voices could be made out on the other side, instead—and far more alarming—were the sinister mechanical rumblings that were growing louder by the second. The walls vibrated and small pieces of plaster fell from the ceiling. Metal objects rattled on the shelves. The Scarab was slowly coming alive—Henry imagined it breathing—and both he and Mr Skinner sensed it gathering power to itself like some ancient god awoken after languishing for centuries in dark and dust.

Deciding it was unsafe to remain a moment longer, Mr Skinner pulled Henry away.

'Come on, Henry, let's make ourselves scarce!'

They ran back to where Kit waited with Carpet unrolled, jumped aboard and before they knew it they were streaking past the doors out into the night—Tita a few inches behind on her broom.

Outside, the spell binding the fog was dissolving fast and the city reappeared from the gloom, street by street. Kit wheeled Carpet around and stopped in mid-air and Tita came up to hover alongside. As she did, they were startled by an almighty explosion, that lit up the sky.

Dry heat gusted into their faces and shockwaves slopped the air. Then, briefly, it rained bricks.

Kit steadied Carpet and peered over the side. Not a trace of the workshop remained and he shouted out for them to see the reason why.

A black monster was slowly pulling itself out of the wreckage, a black unshiny monster that resembled a new-born creature hatching from a shell, its legs heaving off fragments of shattered wall and roof; hauling its bulk into the open for the very first time.

To begin with there was so much dust and debris it was difficult to see, but once the Scarab had crawled free of the ruin every detail grew horribly clear. The two tall smoke stacks belched out clouds of filthy smoke and sparks, and the machine's head moved constantly, scanning the night with powerful beams emitted from a pair of burning pink eyes. Its antennae twitched backwards and forwards, sometimes separately, sometimes together, and when least expected they let loose a burst of rattling gunfire, glowing red hot in the darkness.

Mr Skinner, frowning, studied the machine's every movement.

'Kit,' he said at last, 'I've an idea how the Scarab may work. To prove if I'm right or not, I want you to make something drop from the sky close to where the Scarab's beams will pick it up.'

'What sort of thing d'you mean?' asked Kit puzzled.

'Anything, so long as it's able to be detected but won't be missed if never seen again.'

Kit cast Henry a what-on-earth-can-this-be-about? look then moved his hands in enchantment. Threads of mist rose rapidly from the remaining banks of fog and were woven swiftly together until there was a patch of darkness similar to a tiny storm cloud. Kit worked upon it with his magic as if modelling a lump of shapeless clay, and

157

suddenly Henry saw what he was making—an almost life-sized dragon, back arched and tail coiled, tilting down from the sky.

'Allow me,' said Tita, adding a sparkle to the shadow dragon's eyes. That really brought it to life.

Finally done, Kit let go of his creation and it began to tip forward under its own weight as if pouncing on Luca, its front paws spread to crush the Scarab beneath its claws.

But the Scarab had different ideas. As the shadow dragon slowly descended towards it, twin beams of pink light greedily fixed it in their sight—for a second—then two cannons upon the Scarab's armoured back swivelled abruptly in the same direction. Hardly had they stopped than the firing started and the air was rocked by explosions, ripping the shadow dragon apart until not a breath of it remained.

Afterwards the air rolled, and Carpet and Tita rode it up and down like a powerful swell. Henry took his fingers from his ears.

'Has it stopped?' he asked meekly.

'Just as I thought,' said Mr Skinner, but with only a small degree of satisfaction. 'The Scarab reacts to movement—the bigger the movement the greater the fire in return.'

'You mean we could be in danger?' said Tita.

Mr Skinner shook his head. 'I don't think so, we're not in range. If we were we would have been blasted out of the sky long before now.'

He sounded horribly matter of fact about it.

'What about those witches there?' said Henry suddenly nodding across to three witches flying in to investigate the explosions, hair and robes flying raggedly.

Mr Skinner stiffened, his face creased with concern. Then he started to shout at the top of his voice.

'Go back—go back, I say!'

Henry and Tita, swept up by his urgency, shouted with him; Kit jumped to his feet and waved his arms. But the witches were simply too preoccupied to notice. Ah . . . but the Scarab noticed *them*. Its head turned sharply, sweeping its beaming eyes skywards—the antennae-rifles moving just a fraction of a second behind. Gunfire rang out. Shot flew up in a line of white-hot dots.

Seeing the danger at last, two of the witches managed to dive to safety. The third was less lucky. She slumped forward on her broom and went hurtling down, crashing into a roof.

Dodging further gunfire bursts the two other witches flocked back to her, leaping off their brooms when still fully ten feet in the air, and landing beside the injured witch as lightly as stepping off a kerb. Immediately they set to work, one taking herbs from a pouch, the other crooning charms to clot the blood.

'Come on, there may be something we can do to help too,' said Kit; and when the detective shot him a look, added angrily, 'You want us to stay here and not do nothing at all, Mr Skinner? Don't worry about the Scarab, I'll be careful, I'll fly us in low.'

He urged Carpet forward, steadying it from time to time because Carpet was woven for speed not caution. And as they slunk between roofs it was to the sound of distant explosions or sudden flashes of blood red light which marked the Scarab's destructive progress; while many fires had sprung up in the wreckage it left behind, flames leaping through holes in shattered roofs, the air acrid with smoke. Getting closer, Tita realized that one of the two tending witches was her mother. Before she could call out to her, a mob of angry birds flew up in their faces, shrieking an alarm. Margha Stara glared up savagely until she recognized them, then she raced up on her broomstick.

159

'Molda Lup is badly wounded,' she said at once, tears streaming down her face and dripping freely off her chin.

'We saw it happen,' admitted Mr Skinner. 'And I'll tell you now, Margha Stara, unless you warn your people to keep their heads low many more will end up like her—the Scarab is designed to seek out and destroy anything that moves.'

Margha Stara nodded her understanding and growing more firm with herself wiped her nose on her sleeve.

'I'll tell them,' she said. 'But we cannot force the ordinary folk to stay inside their houses. Already there is so much panic.'

She paused as a particularly large explosion drowned out her words, setting her birds screaming and pulling out their own feathers in terror.

'But magic . . . ' said Kit impatiently. 'It can't be totally useless against that thing—can it?'

Margha Stara cast him a weary look, her face seeming so much older. 'There is nothing we can do,' she said starkly. 'Absolutely nothing. I have never known anything so heavily guarded against enchantment.'

'She's right,' agreed Mr Skinner. 'Still, we must do as best we can the little that we *can* do. Margha Stara, will you fly me to the palace? The king is in more danger than he realizes and I shall breathe more easily once he is safely away from his uncle's assassins.'

'Certainly. Climb behind me, Mr Skinner, I will take you wherever you wish to go.'

'Mama—' began Tita.

'Don't worry, child, I promise to bear Mr Skinner's warning in mind and keep well out of the machine's sight. Are you ready, Mr Skinner?'

Mr Skinner awkwardly exchanged the flying-carpet for the witch's narrow broom handle, making it clumsily obvious he had never ridden by broom before. The broom

160

sank by several inches and when he was sufficiently settled Margha Stara turned to the others.

'Listen to me, you three children, and listen well,' she said. 'Although you may think it some kind of great adventure, the city is no place for you, there are far too many dangers. The minute I leave with Mr Skinner, I want you to go straight back to Mountain Tree. Yes—yes, never mind those sulky looks, Tita, you can make yourselves useful *there*—preparing healing charms and as many cobweb bandages as you can make. Tell the old witches who have stayed behind to help you, tell them to milk the spiders for their thread. If it is as I fear we shall need their healing magic like never before.'

With these grim words and her eyes gleaming with tears she kicked her broom and dived into a dark alley, Mr Skinner gripping her waist for dear life, and birds flanking them upon either side.

Kit watched until they had disappeared from sight.

'Go back and make bandages out of spiders' webs with a bunch of ol' grannies—huh, is that all?' he said in disgust.

'What else can we do?' asked Henry suddenly distracted by a flare of white, jagged edged light. 'Heavens, look! The palace is under attack.'

A roof of blue glazed tiles disintegrated beneath a cloud of dirty smoke; and across the face of the palace they saw two pink beams move restlessly back and forth, the flutter of an innocent banner enough to unleash a new round of cannon fire.

Soon thick clouds of smoke poured from a number of gaping holes. Above them, serene and strangely undamaged, stood the astrological clock whose gilded face gleamed unnaturally in the wild advancing firelight.

Suddenly and for no earthly reason Henry could make out, Kit gave an excited yell and turned to him and Tita, his eyes shining.

'What would you say if I told you the maddest idea has just sprung into my head?'

'Nothing at all,' groaned Henry. 'I shouldn't be the slightest bit surprised.'

'What is it?' asked Tita.

'I'll explain when there's more time,' said Kit. 'But first we have to reach the palace while there's still any of it left standing.'

He ordered Carpet to follow the trail of Margha Stara's broom, and it immediately plunged them into some of the narrowest, darkest alleys to be found anywhere in Luca. On corners, people huddled in confused groups waiting for the latest news. Tita shouted at them to go back into their homes and stay there. Seeing her broomstick, their eyes rounded in terror and they fled, some pausing long enough to throw a stone. None struck, but Tita was hurt considerably more to find herself so feared and despised.

'I was only trying to help them,' she said, sadly shaking her head.

'I know . . . don't worry,' said Kit kindly. 'After tonight the truth about magic is bound to come out. You wait, soon they'll be cheering their heads off at every enchanter they see.'

'Huh, I'll believe that when it happens,' said Tita.

'Of course it will. Now cheer up, we're nearly there.'

And so they arrived at the palace—upon a side as yet undamaged by the Scarab's constant bombardment. There was no sign of Margha Stara and Mr Skinner, which Kit thought as well considering the three of them had no right to be there.

They flew up quickly and once at roof level saw the palace in flames. Kit landed in a courtyard unchoked by smoke and looked behind for Tita. She had landed safely and was flicking curls of ash from her long hair, but as they dropped as thickly as black snowflakes she soon gave up trying.

Pausing only to roll up Carpet, Kit hurried them towards the crackle of flames. Everywhere they went lay in complete chaos. Endless panicked servants dashed past, each carrying something, as ants do when their nest is broken into—a salvaged oil painting or French clock in this case; some carried a meagre leather bucket of water to douse the flames—most of which got spilt as they ran.

Tita thought she at last understood. 'Is that why you brought us here?' she asked Kit. 'To help fight the fire with our magic.'

'No, first there is something more important than that,' said Kit. 'I think I remember the way from here—watch out for flying glass, though.'

He ran down a smoke-filled corridor, side-stepping a band of wigless and sooty-faced servants who, like madmen stealing washing, were frantically ripping tapestries from the walls.

'Here,' said Kit at last, after several more twists and turns brought them out by a small insignificant door.

'Why here?' demanded Henry.

'Because this is the place I saw him last and I've a sneaking suspicion he was trying to build himself a nest. If he was and our luck holds he should still be around.'

Henry stared at him in disbelief. 'I thought so—you're talking about that nasty little gremlin creature, aren't you? Oh, Kit! How can you possibly think that worth risking our lives for? It probably won't be a bit grateful for it—you see, it'll turn around and bite us all for being such complete idiots and you know what, it'll be right.'

'Henry, I know what I'm doing,' said Kit patiently. 'Help me, that's all I ask—you too, Tita. Luddite may not be specially bright but he's wary of magic and that's the

163

only way I see us catching him now—oh, and please don't hurt him.'

'Don't hurt *him*,' muttered Tita under her breath as Kit tugged open the door and sent a glow-ball on ahead.

They entered the clock's shadowy innards, or rather the wreckage of what they used to be.

Tita gazed around and gasped. 'Kit, we've come too late,' she whispered. 'The tower's had a direct hit from one of the Scarab's guns.'

Kit smiled. 'I don't think so, more likely it's a direct hit from Luddite's rage . . . I'll look over in the corner.'

Henry, out of sorts and feeling uncooperative, picked his way through a pile of broken cogs.

'Well, what does this *gremlin* thing look like—' he began only to break off with a piercing yell. 'Kit! Kit! Quick! Something's jumped on my back.' He squealed and danced around in horror.

'Oh good work, Henry, you've found him,' cried Kit looking across and beaming with delight.

'*Found it*—the little murderer is attacking me!' bawled Henry.

'Oh no, you're quite wrong, Henry. Luddite isn't attacking you—he's just frightened by the loud bangs, that's all. Hold still a minute.'

'But its claws are digging into me—Ow! Ow!'

With great difficulty Kit managed to spin Henry around and put a finger and thumb upon Luddite's neck. He squeezed gently. Instantly the gremlin dropped into his arms, heavy, spiky, and deep in an enchanted sleep.

Kit smiled at Henry's dark scowling face as he rubbed his shoulders. 'There, that wasn't so hard, was it?' he said.

Remembering the savage bite received at their last meeting, Tita studied the gremlin from a wary distance. 'So now we have it, what happens next?' she asked.

164

Kit grew a little more serious. 'Next comes the really difficult part,' he said. 'And I don't think we'll be able to manage it on our own. We need to find Mr Skinner.'

# Chapter Fifteen

They slipped away from the palace shortly after, Kit carefully cradling the sleeping gremlin in his cloak, and Henry still complaining about the sharpness of his brass claws. Strangely, not once had anyone challenged them, even though Tita with her broom was so obviously a witch; and it required hardly much extra thought to work out that the rolled up carpet beneath Kit's arm was more than likely a flying variety—making him a wizard. But then nobody had much time for thought—servants ran shrieking, trying to rescue what they could—so for all the attention they received, Kit and his friends might well have imagined themselves invisible.

With not a single head turned, they flew up and away relying on the same route by which they had arrived, and which remained fairly safe from the Scarab's rampaging. This did not mean that the Scarab had ground to a halt, worse luck. Quite the opposite in fact. The sound of exploding shells came thicker than ever, but this was because the enchanters led by Margha Stara had begun to play a deadly game with it.

Believing it best to keep the Scarab and its havoc contained in one small part of the city—at the base of the palace—rather than let it loose to roam wherever it pleased, they used themselves as human targets; so that every time the Scarab looked set to break out into one of the surrounding streets, they'd lure it back by suddenly darting up on their brooms.

So far this ploy had worked well for them but the cost to

that particular quarter of the city was high. The palace and buildings round about were shattered and burning. Many of the palace's gilded rooms gaped open, with furniture about to topple over the brink; and a steeple hung upside down, a few groaning timbers away from crashing to earth. And still the Scarab's angry pink beams showed not the slightest sign of dimming, its mandibles angrily crunching trees in half if they got in its way; its cannons rarely silent.

To the distant sound of explosions, Kit steered Carpet around the metal brute, giving it a wide berth and keeping to the lesser alleys which were narrow and safe; while Tita on her broom called across to every witch they met for news of her mother and Mr Skinner, but no one could tell them where they were.

In the end the problem was solved for them. From out of the darkness one of Margha Stara's eagles swooped down and seized a handful of Tita's long hair and began to drag her along by it. Tita screamed, but the eagle's talons remained tightly clenched.

'Shoo—shoo, you great feathered duster,' called Henry waving his arms.

'Henry, this is an eagle—the king of birds—not a common little cockney sparrow,' sighed Kit.

'Ow—he's right,' said Tita. 'It's too proud to give me up. I'll just have to let it take me where it wants—all right, stop pulling, you brute, I'm coming—I'm coming!'

Carpet and the two boys followed after her and their insistent eagle guide. Altogether they made a strange procession. The eagle, growing no more gentle with Tita, led them to a sheltered valley formed where two roofs met. There, clinging to the slope of one roof was Mr Skinner, Margha Stara, and a host of wizards and witches, as well as King Eugen trembling in a blanket. At their feet a small flock of birds cowered, frightened and bad-tempered, shuddering at the sound of every new explosion.

Having done its work, the eagle finally let go of Tita's hair and hopped down to greet its mate, giving her a soft peck and nuzzle. It was the only affectionate greeting to be had.

Mr Skinner threw the newcomers a cool, unsurprised glance; his bowler hat was crumpled, his raincoat torn and his glistening face smeared with streaks of dirt. But if he were cool, Margha Stara was anything but. She blew up in a furious temper, made worse after Tita ill-advisedly complained about how she had been treated by her mother's bird.

'Count yourself lucky I do not fly down there and pull out your hair myself, you wicked, wicked disobedient girl,' blazed the witch, so angry that every other word sparked. 'Why don't you ever listen? Why do you have to keep breaking my heart? I told you to be gone from the city—fly, I said—yet you deliberately chose to stay and defy me—*me* your own mother. And don't you ever—*ever*—again say anything harsh about a bird of mine, my girl, at least *they* know how to obey me. Not like you, Tita! They don't risk their lives playing silly games.'

'Not games, Mama,' said Tita quietly defiant.

'We've come to give you this,' added Kit hastily. He held out Luddite who at that moment looked particularly unimpressive, his mouth dropping open in a snore.

Mr Skinner was puzzled. He reached out and touched the sleeping creature but withdrew his hand almost at once. 'Its fur feels as sharp as brass tacks,' he marvelled.

'Most gremlin fur does,' said Kit, and quickly he explained his plan to use the talents of the machine hating gremlin to destroy the Scarab.

When he was done he half expected everyone to be so happy that they would sing his praises in loud voices, but instead Mr Skinner didn't look at all like singing; he looked extremely doubtful.

'The gremlin?' he said.

Kit stared at him, annoyed. 'Well? You got summat better to offer?'

The detective was forced to admit he hadn't, but he still couldn't see how Kit's plan could be made to work. To prove his point he swiftly pulled himself up to the top of the roof and studied the Scarab through his binoculars for several long minutes before sliding back to report.

'Sorry, Kit, I'm afraid your idea falls at the first hurdle,' he said. 'Apart from the two smoke stacks I can see no other opening in the Scarab's armour. Small though it is, it's impossible to get that creature inside.'

'Oh,' said Kit his face dropping disappointedly. And that might have been an end to it had not Henry sprung heroically to his rescue.

'Surely, Mr Skinner,' he said, 'if there is smoke there must be fire. And for fire to burn, the flames need air. And if there is no air vent on the top it is only reasonable to expect to find one—'

'*Underneath*—of course!' Kit gave a whoop of joy. 'Good old Henry. You know sometimes I think you've far too much brains to be a prince.'

'Thank you, I shall take that as a compliment,' said Henry doubtfully.

Mr Skinner, as pessimistic as ever, saw only the problem of how to flip the Scarab onto its back.

'Magic!' said Kit, amazed that this was a matter for concern.

'Can it be done?' asked Mr Skinner turning to Margha Stara.

She shrugged. 'I don't see why not—not if all our people concentrate their magic at the same time.'

'What we need is some sort of starting signal—something to tell everyone when to begin,' said Tita.

Mr Skinner took out his revolver, checked the chambers of its barrel, then clicked it shut.

'Three shots fired into the air sufficient?' he asked.

'Gunshots—oh yes,' said Tita growing more excited. 'Now hurry, Mama, please. Send out your birds to spread the word. Tell everyone to listen out for Mr Skinner's signal.'

'Child,' said Margha Stara crossly. 'You take too much on yourself. Let your mother and your elders make the decisions from now on; you just be sure to follow what we say.'

'Sorry, Mama,' said Tita well and truly put in her place.

Margha Stara spoke to her birds . . . She closed her eyes and every bird immediately swivelled round its head towards her, eyes gleaming sharply. They listened intently while Margha Stara spoke—but not with her tongue— and Kit wondered what magic he was witnessing; whether it was mind-walking or some other form of magic, perhaps one which used the tiny hummingbird familiar as a go-between. Whatever it was, the moment she opened her eyes the birds flew off, each paired with its mate: some flying to the left and some flying to the right, but none flying higher than the roof tops.

They were gone for only a brief time and Margha Stara made sure to count the pairs as they flew back. When satisfied every bird had returned safely, she climbed up to the roof ridge where the older enchanters had already gathered, but not Kit and his friends. She refused to let the youngsters join them.

'Please, Mama,' begged Tita. 'It's too cruel making us stay down here on our own.'

'Hmph.'

'It's not like we're much use standing about jus' twiddling our thumbs,' said Kit.

Mr Skinner glanced down and took pity on them. 'Oh . . . let them come, Margha Stara.'

'Mmm . . . very well, if they must. But they have to do everything they are told. *Everything*. You hear me, Tita? You hear what I say, my girl?'

Kit grinned at Tita. Leaving Carpet and Luddite beside the terrified king, he scrambled up and found a good position next to a wizard in a purple robe.

On his other side was Henry, and Kit had to smile. Henry was feeling and acting all important because it had been decided he could be look-out. He watched through Mr Skinner's Royal Air Army issue binoculars, but there was little for him to report. The Scarab had paused and for the moment was silent, its pink beams scanning the rubble for the slightest movement.

'We wait for your signal, Mr Skinner,' whispered Margha Stara.

Slowly the detective raised his arm. He fired once . . . twice . . . three times.

Then the mass enchantment began.

Some enchanters like Margha Stara pointed with wands of ancient wood; many more preferred to let their magic pour out of them straight through their hands. But together they turned the air electric, making it crackle like half formed thunderbolts—and swirl and thicken so that everything was slightly out of focus; at the same time, Kit found the discharge of magic had caused his unruly hair to stand on end.

Henry, glued to the binoculars, saw the Scarab suddenly lurch as the invisible wave of magic struck its side without, so far as he could see, inflicting so much as the tiniest dent. Yet one of the machine's eyes flickered momentarily then blazed out angrily again; and the rifle fire that was spat out peppered the darkness at random.

'It's beginning to tip on its side!' shouted Henry, who

then found the binoculars snatched off him by Mr Skinner who wanted to see for himself.

'Excellent,' he muttered.

Even at a distance they heard the screech and hammering of metal—but at a cost, for there was not a witch or wizard who was not feeling a great strain on their power, Kit amongst them. He sensed his magic draining out of him like water from a cracked jug. He gasped for breath and sweat trickled down the side of his face.

'Just a little more, Kit,' urged Henry, who was helpless to do anything else.

Kit shut his eyes. He was beginning to hurt inside as if from a bad case of stomach cramps. He knew his magic was coming to an end. Next to him, Henry suddenly sucked in his breath.

'Oh, well done, Kit,' he exclaimed. 'The monster's fallen—it's gone right over!'

'Thank goodness,' groaned Kit.

He closed his hand to stem the flow of magic and the pain vanished at once. When he opened his eyes he saw Henry smiling and Mr Skinner passed him the binoculars. The Scarab lay on its back, legs hanging awkward and crooked and perfectly still. Seeing it like this, a group of young wizards jumped up and cheered.

Henry was delighted too. 'What d'you know,' he laughed. 'We shan't be needing the services of that nasty little gremlin after all by the looks of things. The Scarab's no different to any other beetle—put it on its back and it dies.'

'I'm afraid not,' said Mr Skinner bleakly.

Henry looked again. To his dismay he saw one of the Scarab's metal legs give a violent twitch. The movement was deliberate and not at all the final shudder of a machine as it died. In careful stages the leg jerked downwards until it made contact with the ground, then the clawed foot

172

scrabbled briefly for grip and was still. After this the middle leg on the same side did likewise, followed by the third and final leg.

'Oh no, after all that effort it's going to right itself,' said Tita.

Further along, those enchanters who thought the battle over and won dived for cover, their cheering ceased.

Mr Skinner peered through his binoculars. 'You were right, Henry, there *is* an air vent underneath,' he said.

Hearing this, Kit felt a jolt go through him. He knew he had to do something before it was too late—even if it ended in dismal failure. At least that was better than doing nothing at all. And so slithering down the roof he scooped up Luddite and kicked open Carpet.

'Sorry, Carpet,' he said leaping upon it; and it rose at once, without command, because it sensed his urgency.

'No, Kit—wait!' shouted Mr Skinner.

But nothing could stop Kit now, not Mr Skinner nor Margha Stara with a whole band of enchanters behind her; nor even the Scarab, which as yet could not turn its head and mark him with its murderous beams (but how long before it was back on its wheels and able to do so?). Kit refused to let himself think about anything so unsettling, fixing his mind on what lay ahead in the next few minutes.

He swept down upon the half raised Scarab, blood or magic pounding in his ears. He saw the vent clearly it was the only opening there was.

'Hover!' he commanded, and Carpet hung so still that not a single thread quivered in its fringe.

There wasn't a moment to waste. The Scarab was determinedly inching itself up on its three spindly legs: it wouldn't be long before its balance shifted and it hammered down upon its wheels—back to how it was with nothing gained. Narrowing his eyes Kit studied the vent. It was small but just about large enough to take a creature of Luddite's size. Leaning out from Carpet as far as he dared he pushed the gremlin into the opening head first.

'Wake up, boy,' he whispered encouragingly. 'Time to go to work, so go on, be a pal. Do your very worst.'

He heard Luddite give a wakening growl and then was gone, scrabbling deeper inside.

A good job for Kit he did, he had such little time left: the Scarab had raised itself exactly on its side and was poised to come down with the very next push. From the front arose a mechanical whirring. The head struggled to turn.

'Go!' shouted Kit at his flying-carpet. As it jerked into motion, the Scarab finally over-balanced and came crashing down, missing him by inches; while the pink beams—back in operation—swept towards him followed by the antennae rifles, a new round of ammunition clicking into position.

Kit prayed for a miracle and his prayer was answered. The whole fiery sky suddenly seemed to burst open and be full of birds of every kind—eagles, harriers, and sparrow-hawks all swooping in; while a group of buzzards wheeled more cautiously then circled down together. Next came the crows, rooks, and magpies, none of which had the same lightning speed, but they more than made up for it by their sheer numbers and overwhelming noise; and the owls followed silently behind, as ghosts are bound to follow the living.

Of course this was no happy accident. Kit guessed that Margha Stara had sent them to confuse the Scarab and confuse it they did. But as the guns blazed, half a dozen birds dropped to the ground and lay there, each a lifeless heap of crumpled feathers—the poor brave things having sacrificed themselves for Kit, giving him the precious seconds he needed to return to the roof where his friends waited.

Henry was overjoyed. He squeezed Kit's arm until it hurt. 'You did it—you did it, Kit! But I could hardly bear to watch,' he said.

Mr Skinner patted Kit warmly on the back. 'A sterling job, son. I only hope your gremlin turns out half as pugnacious.'

Kit smiled modestly and wondered what *pugnacious* meant.

At the roof ridge everyone gathered hoping to spot some indication that the Scarab was weakening. But beam and cannon followed each other very much like before.

'Come on, Luddite,' willed Kit. 'You've proved you're a nasty little thing eaten up with hate, show us what you think of ol' Mr Sparks and his invention. Don't be shy, boy, you can do it—I just know you can.'

Luddite didn't disappoint.

Suddenly a cloud of powdery white smoke blasted from the smoke stacks, and with it came a peculiar high-pitched whistling sound.

Kit laughed approvingly. 'Ah, this is starting to look the business,' he said.

He laughed again when moments later one of the beams went out; and Tita who had the binoculars reported that the other eye was constantly changing colour.

Yet binoculars were hardly necessary to know that the Scarab was decidedly unwell. It moved back and forth aimlessly, as did the silent rows of cannon. For no good reason the two telescopic antennae kept shooting out and shrinking back and its one working eye, as Tita had observed, kept flickering to green.

Kit never thought it possible but in a complete turn around in events the Scarab was changing from a monstrous metal brute into something . . . dare he say it?

175

. . . something quite comical, and he took wicked pleasure in watching it happen. Everything was going haywire. Why, now its legs were waving out of control, crashing down or kicking and gouging each other with their claws. Oh, how the sparks flew . . . Turning to Henry, Kit shared a grin with him and Henry grinned back no less generously.

And as they watched, laughing and pointing things out to each other, a familiar character made a brief reappearance, darting between the Scarab's wheels; his thick fur black and oily and standing on end. It was Luddite (who else?) and as if trying to outrun his own shadow he streaked across to the nearest ruined building and was lost from sight.

Guessing the reason the gremlin had 'abandoned ship', Mr Skinner startled everyone with his barked command. 'Heads down—now!'

'Why?' Henry made the mistake of asking. Prince or not, Mr Skinner grabbed him by the collar and pulled him roughly away. Together they rolled to the bottom of the roof.

'Mr Skinner *really*,' cried Henry, his face crimson. But before he could examine his newly acquired grazes, a spectacular explosion rocked the air and made the building shake beneath them. Little twisted pieces of red hot metal clattered down from the sky; one burnt a hole in Margha Stara's gown, another singed Carpet which jumped in surprise.

Afterwards an eerie silence fell. Kit, burning with curiosity, was the first to break it.

'D'you think it is safe to go up and take a look now?' he whispered.

Mr Skinner hesitated then gave a nod and Kit was off up the roof like a cat after a pigeon. What he saw when he reached the top cheered him immensely.

The Scarab was no more and in its place was a deep blackened crater that smouldered and glowed.

'Wow,' said Henry coming up behind.

A faint ripple of a cheer broke out as others crept from hiding and saw the sight for themselves. The ripples swiftly joined together and grew louder until everyone was shouting at the tops of their voices; and witches and wizards flew up on their brooms, looping the loop and no longer afraid.

Margha Stara cried and laughed by turn. She hugged everyone and kissed Mr Skinner so violently that his bowler hat was knocked off (afterwards he retrieved it sheepishly, a hand on his head trying to hide his bald patch) and all the birds squawked, screamed, rasped, or whistled.

It was an absolute madhouse.

And then, quite unexpectedly, it started to snow—great fat flakes drifting from the sky

'But . . . but that's ridiculous,' said Tita staring up, the snow flecking her dark hair. 'It never snows in Callalabasa—not even in winter!'

'Magical transmutation,' remarked Kit casually.

'What?'

'We did it at Eton in weather-control. When there's a large discharge of magic it can affect the weather. *Magical transmutation*. Foggy Fogetty told us that after the Battle of Wands and Black Cats, it rained herring for three days solid.'

'I expect the black cats appreciated it,' laughed Henry.

And the three of them stood close together in the thick falling snow, laughing and feeling dizzy with happiness; and no one noticed that the long night was over and dawn had come.

177

# Chapter Sixteen

Word spread slowly that the battle had ended and that Luca's streets were again safe to walk. Throughout the morning hours frightened families were to be seen emerging from cellars and crypts, blinking in the watery grey light. And, depending on exactly whereabouts in the city they reappeared, there was something to make every mouth drop open in awe— whether it was a burnt-out building, or a flock of chattering enchanters flying overhead—or simply the snow, the wonderful pure, white snow that covered the ugliest of the city's scars and made everything so calm and silent.

With the main danger gone, the fires were swiftly brought under control, the enchanters using magic alongside the ordinary folk who ran to fill buckets at the wells. But magic proved more effective by far. And when folk saw this, and saw how the enchanters gave help to those hurt and in need whoever they were, some old prejudices fell away. It was a first step towards the day folk finally painted over the horrible staring eyes that glared out at each other over every doorway.

Meantime Kit, Henry, and Tita found they had attracted a small band of hostile-looking urchins who kept staring across at Tita's broom.

'What's the matter with them?' said Tita irritably. 'Do they think because of my magic I have two heads or my fingers are webbed?'

The situation seemed set to worsen when a dark-eyed

boy stepped forward and shouted 'Witch!' and his hand rose as if about to make the sign against evil—

But he didn't. Instead he hurled a snowball which exploded in a puff of powder against Henry's ear.

'Ow! Little brats, don't they know who I am?' cried Henry pompously.

''Course not, Henry,' said Kit. 'That's the point. They don't care who or what we are, they just want some fun.' And scooping up a handful of snow he moulded it quickly and returned fire.

Well, that was the start of a terrific snow fight, snowballs whizzing back and forth; and seeing that Kit and the others were heavily outnumbered, some urchins switched to their side, not knowing that Kit and Tita had already evened things out by making sly use of their magic. That was why their snowballs rarely missed or why they themselves were so hard to hit, while Henry got a complete pasting. Kit hadn't enjoyed himself so much in ages.

Just then, however, Tita gave a warning shout.

'Watch out behind you, Kit!'

'Try to sneak up on me, eh?' said Kit spotting the danger.

An ambusher's snowball did a banana curve around him and missed. Kit pointed. A small but respectable avalanche slid off a nearby roof, catching five urchins at one go, and Kit laughed seeing each urchin briefly turned into a living snowman.

'Though surrounded by his foes, Sir Kit Stixby deals them a deadly blow and lives on to fight another day!'

The battle only ended when Margha Stara swept down on her broom with Mr Skinner perched uncomfortably behind. The band of urchins disappeared at once.

'There you are,' said the witch. Kit guiltily hid a snowball behind his back thinking they were in for a

179

sound telling off, but no, Margha Stara's eyes gleamed approvingly. 'Look at you—I see you *do* know how to behave like ordinary children after all.'

'Yes, Mama,' said Tita grinning.

'Well leave that now and come with us. We are called to the palace. The fires are all out and the assassins arrested, and the king has sent word he wishes to see us.'

Kit shook open Carpet across the snow and Henry followed him aboard, both trying to shake off as much snow as possible. But the cold and wet had already entered Carpet's weave, making it sulky. It showed it by giving them a bumpy ride as they followed last after Tita, rising towards the blackened towers of the palace.

It put down with the two brooms in a snowy courtyard where—as they alighted—theirs were the first sets of prints. Dummock sprang out from behind a pillar, appearing so suddenly he might have been lying in wait for them all night.

'R-uined,' he cried dramatically, throwing up his hands in despair. 'Ab-so-lute-ly *ruined*!'

'What is it, Dummock?' asked Henry.

Dummock stared at him incredulously. 'Why, your clothes, sir, your entire wardrobe of clothes. It will take days to remove the evil reek of smoke. *Days*.'

Kit sniffed at his own sleeve and shrugged. 'The smell don't bother me none,' he said.

Haughtily Dummock sniffed at *him*—all of him—in reproach. 'Well, it bothers *me*,' he said icily and turned on his heels and marched away muttering to himself.

Mr Skinner led the way to King Eugen. The short— usually pleasant—walk had changed into one of sharp contrasts: by turns they were either picking their way through smouldering wreckage or strolling along golden corridors which weren't the slightest bit damaged and might well have been part of a different building. Margha

Stara, who had never before visited the palace, stared around in astonishment at everything.

'Mama, close your mouth,' whispered Tita embarrassed.

'But, child, it's so . . . so . . . ' Margha Stara could not find the words to describe her wonder.

Eventually they reached a long grand room where a gang of mournful servants moved back and forth with dustpans and brushes, noisily sweeping up shards of pointed glass. At the furthest end sat the king surrounded by his ministers, each one of whom had slicked down hair, a little moustache, and a formal black tailcoat. In fact the ministers looked like mirror reflections of each other with not a shoelace difference between them; and Kit couldn't remember the last time he'd seen a more nervous-looking bunch, some ministers shrinking back behind others as Mr Skinner strode up.

The detective removed his bowler hat and they all bowed with different degrees of success—even Margha Stara and Tita, who between them couldn't manage a decent curtsy to save their lives.

When they straightened again, all the ministers were muttering and nudging each other, nobody wanting to be the first to speak. The king began to blush furiously and kept picking at a button.

Finally the under-minister for ponds and watermills gave a cough and said, 'G-gentlemen . . . ' And again less loudly, 'Gentlemen and—and—ha!—ladies too, of course . . . his majesty, King Fugen XIV, wishes it known he has something to say to you.' Then he stopped, suddenly aware that all the other ministers were frowning at him and his outrageous display of forwardness. Some considered him a dangerously ambitious fellow—why in twenty years' time he might even have manoeuvred himself into the job of *first* minister for ponds and watermills. *Disgraceful!*

Slowly the king's mouth opened but for a long time nothing came out. Then—'I . . . ' He stopped to clear his throat. 'I . . . ' he began for a second time before faltering. He closed his eyes. They all leaned forward, waiting. The king took a breath— 'Ijustwanttoexpressmysincerestthanks toyou,allofyou,forwhatyouhavedoneformycountryandI.' He spoke in one breathless rush—then pulled off his button.

'We were glad to do what we could, Majesty,' said Mr Skinner. 'Er . . . may I ask, has there been any fresh news concerning Stafford Sparks and his fellow conspirators?'

The ministers looked at each other, extremely uncomfortable at having to discuss such unpleasant matters. Mr Skinner waited for an answer so the under-minister for ponds and watermills was forced to speak again.

'The Englishman—Stafford Sparks—has vanished—'

'Vanished!' howled Kit, unable to hide his disappointment. 'But you have to go on searching for him. You mustn't give up—'

'As for the others . . . they have been arrested.' The under-minister gave the smallest glimmer of a smile. 'They were found huddled together in a pig sty.'

Tita beamed. 'Good, if nothing else that should teach Señor Pufni what a proper stink should smell like.'

'They were tracked down by police bloodhounds,' continued the under-minister gaining more in confidence. 'Señor Pufni—the former Royal Nose—flew into a rage. He called the dogs *traitors*.'

A dry, wheezy, rarely practised laugh arose from his chest, sounding like a leaky organ. The other ministers stared at him in disgust—the fellow had become a positive egomaniac—and he abruptly fell silent.

'What news about that filthy vampire, Count Drohlomski?' demanded Margha Stara. 'Did he survive the bombardment? If so he deserves to be punished along with the rest for what he did to poor Pampla Droiga.'

'Gone,' whispered the under-minister. 'A hole was blown clean through the dungeon and he took advantage of it to escape.'

'Ha! I hope for his sake you find him before I do,' said the witch looking and sounding so fierce that the ministers drew back in alarm.

Hoping to change the subject, Henry said, 'And your coronation, Majesty, will it still go ahead today as planned?'

The question set every minister violently shaking his head. 'No-no-no-no-no . . . Impossible.'

'The cathedral has a big hole in its dome,' explained the under-minister, 'and the snow has come in. All in all it is neither fit nor safe for such an important ceremony.'

Margha Stara scoffed. 'If that is the only reason, leave it to us enchanters. We will give you a building glorious enough for *an emperor* to be crowned in. It shall be our gift to our new king.'

And again she was so fierce that no one dared refuse her.


After the meeting, Mr Skinner remained behind with the king; and Tita and her mother flew off on their brooms to organize their people. Tita had asked Kit and Henry if they wanted to help them, but Kit had to decline: Carpet was far too damp and needed to dry out a little before any more flying might be considered. It was a lesson he had learnt the hard way. When really wet and in a foul mood because of it, Carpet was inclined to go into spectacular free-fall dives which proved scary even for Kit. Not by pure accident alone were most flying-carpets found in hot dry lands.

So he returned with Henry to his princely room which lay nearby and spread Carpet out in front of the fire. He yawned and stretched before the flames, and turning noticed Henry's bed. The sight of it—so big and soft and comfortable—was too much of a temptation following the previous night's miserable ration of sleep.

'Y'know, Henry,' he said. 'I suddenly feel in desperate need of . . . [yawn] a little nap.'

'Perhaps just forty winks before the coronation,' agreed Henry in a way that showed he had already decided on the same thing.

And so without another word they both crawled onto the feathered mattress that was as wide as a raft, and fell asleep, sleeping more soundly than either had intended, for several hours.

Henry awoke first and gazed around. He slipped from beneath the covers and across the cold marble floor to the balcony and looked out, hugging himself against the icy wind.

'H-Henry?' Kit awoke more sluggishly and for a moment lay wondering where he was until his memory caught up and reminded him.

He sat up rubbing his eyes, his mad hair in a madder tangle than usual. 'Is it still snowing?' he asked indifferently because he could see perfectly well the large silent flakes falling from a lead-grey sky.

'Yes,' replied Henry without turning around. 'Just as well really—come see.'

Pulling a blanket around his shoulders, Kit padded over to join his friend on the balcony. He peered down. What had taken Henry's attention so completely hardly needed pointing out. At the foot of the old palace had arisen a new and equally splendid one, a palace of snow and ice.

Kit gave a long whistle. 'My, that's a piece of magic and no mistake,' he said.

He watched a number of witches and wizards go flittering over the vast expanse of roof, patching and strengthening places where the magic had worn thin.

The whole structure was a gloriously fantastical affair of vaulted roofs and sparkling domes which clustered around each other like a family of snails beneath a stone. Nothing was straight; and put all together it was difficult to take everything in, even after several minutes of trying, for the ice palace spilled into surrounding streets and swept up the sides of existing buildings, half engulfing them in snowdrifts.

It was simply too good not to investigate. Fortunately Carpet was dry enough to fly so Kit and Henry were able to go at once; and finding a triumphant gateway built in massive blocks of clear blue ice they entered the palace, flying over the heads of many of the ordinary people who had flocked there to marvel at the wonders of magic.

They were not alone—Kit was amazed at what had been done in such a relatively short space of time. Flying into the largest of its frost-white halls, he didn't know what impressed him most. Was it the ice columns that held up the roof? Each one was sculptured into the shape of a life-sized tree, with blue flames dancing at the ends of every twig like dazzling blossoms, giving warmth but not melting the snow; while elsewhere in the branches hung the tiniest glow-balls imaginable, like shining berries. Then again perhaps he was more impressed by the monumental ice throne that towered up as tall as a house and was formed by six intertwined ice dragons, the tail of one doubling up as a set of steps leading to a high seat some thirty feet in the air, where the young king would finally and grandly receive his crown.

'At least no one should have any trouble in following what's going on,' observed Henry.

Just then a voice shouted up at them, and looking

185

down, Kit saw Margha Stara, Mr Skinner, and Tita; Kit waved and ordered Carpet to land.

'Well, what do you think?' asked Tita running across and clearly expecting a compliment.

'About what?' Kit made an act out of looking around. 'Oh, you mean *this*? Oh yeah, I've just noticed it. Won't be half bad once it gets finished.'

Henry elbowed him in the ribs. 'Ignore him, I think it is simply splendid,' he said far more graciously.

Looking across, the word *splendid* might also be applied to Margha Stara just then; for as she spoke privately with Mr Skinner she was surrounded by a flock of little black terns, which darted around her so close and swift that they gave the impression she was robed in a living coat of wings. At her ear the tiny hummingbird glowed with a tropical brilliance strangely out of place in a house of snow and ice.

'Come on, I've saved you some seats,' said Tita grabbing Kit and Henry by their arms and dragging them across to a pair of empty ice chairs. Each chair had either boy's name deep inside the ice.

'I did that,' said Tita proudly.

'Won't we need a cushion . . . or something?' murmured Henry.

Tita laughed. 'Don't worry, the ice isn't chilly. You won't catch a cold.'

'Thank goodness for that,' said Henry remembering, all at the same time, past coronations, past hard chairs in draughty corners, and past coughs and sneezes the morning after.

The ice palace was filling up fast—ordinary folk and enchanters rubbing shoulders with the more expected prime ministers, ambassadors, and archdukes. The ceremony was promising to be a lot less stuffy than it would have been had it gone ahead in the cathedral as planned; and when Kit wondered what it most reminded him of, he decided it was a school rugby match in the excited minutes up to the moment when the referee blew his whistle for start of play. Flocks of enchanters had taken up grandstand positions in the branches of the ice trees; their legs hung down untidily and they called across to each other from different trees. It was unspeakably noisy.

Suddenly trumpets sounded a brassy fanfare and all lively chatter dwindled away; the air became heavy with incense. Archbishop Constantin entered dressed in his golden robes, followed by King Eugen and then a whole host of choirboys (the one who stuck out his tongue at Kit had cause to regret it when Kit retaliated and stung him with a mild curse). The king looked around him bewildered—lost in a long ermine train, which gave him the appearance of a naughty schoolboy caught playing a dressing-up game in his father's best clothes. As he approached the throne, the archbishop sang in a deep ponderous voice and swung the heavy smouldering incense burner on the end of its chain; the choir sang and then—

Well, for Kit *nothing*. After fifteen minutes of trying to follow what was going on he grew bored and nodded off. He awoke with a start right at the very end, as the whole congregation joined voices to cry, 'Long live the king!'

The king in question blushed furiously beneath the polished gold of his crown.

'May he make a good king for *all* of his people,' wished Margha Stara firmly.

'I think he will,' said Mr Skinner. 'He has a lot to learn but I do believe his heart is in the right place.'

Suddenly delighted oohs and ahhs broke out across the hall, revealing that the feast had arrived, the kitchens having miraculously survived from the night before. Henry

187

stared greedily at the mounting piles of food, much of it assembled into fantastic displays—sailing ships, flocks of swans, and glittering coats of arms.

'Good,' he said. 'Coronations always make me hungry.'

'Henry, since when did you need an excuse to scoff?' sighed Kit, but Henry's mouth was already too full to answer.

The feast was in full swing when a small vaguely familiar figure appeared and made his way up to Henry and Mr Skinner; yet it was only after he had brushed the snow off himself that they fully recognized him as Captain Lamb from the *Flying George*. He looked serious.

'Confounded snow,' he said as if this explained matters sufficiently. 'Not on me, sir,' he said seeing Henry stare at him blankly. 'On the *Flying George*. If it gets any thicker it'll crash down like an overladen branch. I'm afraid we must leave at once.'

'*Leave*,' lamented Henry loudly. 'I was just starting to enjoy myself!' And Kit smiled noticing him fill his pockets with pastries.

'If you like, Mr Skinner, I'll fly you there on the back of my broom,' offered Margha Stara.

'And, Captain, you can come with us,' said Kit.

This was quickly settled, although Henry couldn't help thinking some small matter overlooked.

'Dummock!' he cried suddenly. 'Don't forget him. He's up at the palace, no doubt elbow deep in washing suds.'

'I'll fetch Dummock,' said Tita. 'He can ride on my broom behind me.'

'Now that,' said Henry with a wicked gleam in his eye, 'is something I can't wait to see.'

There then followed a frenzied round of farewells—to wizards, witches, generals, a minister or two, and finally a king. Kit was also glad to see Voma Taslavia and Bahbu again. They crept up shyly and she touched his hand and smiled, before they contentedly melted back into the crowds.

'To broom!' yelled Margha Stara deciding that the farewells had gone on quite long enough.

Her broom rose heavily, still not accustomed to the weight of an extra passenger; and Carpet was no less heavy and sluggish for the same reason. Outside they waited in the snow for Tita who had shot off to find Dummock. She reappeared very slowly with the manservant rigid with terror behind.

'But, Prince—your luggage!' he wailed.

'Blow the luggage,' said Henry carelessly. 'It can be sent on later.'

Dummock gave a moan of unhappiness, and they set off through the swirling snow. Indeed the snow came at them so thickly that they couldn't make out the old tower and royal airship until practically on top of them both; the *Flying George* the only craft still moored there. Kit heard its engines first, then saw a long grey shape. The engines were running in readiness for a quick departure, but as yet each snowy propeller lay still. Behind them, about the tail, exhaust fumes formed a billowing white cloud; and electric lights shone welcomingly at the portholes. As Captain Lamb had stated, the top half of the royal airbarge was thickly encrusted with snow and most of the crew were gathered on the tower trying desperately to knock it off with a variety of long-handled brushes, two men to a brush.

Gliding in on a single breath of wind, Carpet and the two brooms landed right in the middle of this hectic scene. As soon as his feet touched firm stone, Dummock fled up the gangway like a cat let out of a box, his face pale and a hand pressed to his mouth.

'Leave that now, men,' Captain Lamb told his crew. 'Get ready to cast off, we're going home.'

189

*Home*, thought Kit. It made him feel strange inside but in a nice warming way, like a sip of hot chocolate by a winter's fire.

However if he expected to slip away with a wave and a polite smile he was very much mistaken. Seizing him in a bear-hug, Margha Stara kissed him over and over on the forehead and ruffled his hair—then hugged whoever else came near her, including one or two astonished crewmen who just happened to be hurrying past.

In a way that was far easier than saying goodbye to Tita: in recent days they had become such close friends, and saying goodbye to a friend is never easy.

Henry shook her hand very formally. 'If ever you come to England . . . '

'Yes,' said Tita staring down.

'We can show you the sights, then you can meet our gang,' said Kit. 'I'm sure they'll like you.'

She nodded and smiled briefly. 'Who knows, perhaps you and Henry will even return to Callalabasa . . . one day.'

'One day . . . perhaps.'

Kit crouched down and carefully rolled up Carpet. Then Mr Skinner crossed over and put his hands on the boys' shoulders. 'We ought to go aboard,' he said, 'or Captain Lamb will set sail without us. Goodbye, Margha Stara. Goodbye, Tita.'

He led Kit and Henry up the gangplank. They climbed very slowly, pausing twice to turn back and wave. And once safely aboard, the three of them found portholes where they could continue waving. Margha Stara was crying, Tita was struggling not to.

Then, once the gangway was lifted and the door secured, Mr Skinner made his way to the bridge. Soon after, the engines steady thrum accelerated to a straining roar, and one by one the propellers spluttered into life.

They drove the snow into a stinging blizzard; Margha
Stara and Tita all but swallowed up by it, their hair
whipping wildly.

'Goodbye, Tita!' shouted Kit one last time—then they
were gone.

Henry gave a deep sigh and collapsed into the soft
leather of a windowside armchair.

'Why is it that goodbyes make me feel so sad that I
get ravenously hungry?'

Kit lobbed a banana at him from a bowl heavy with
fruit.

Henry started to peel it then thrust it aside. 'It's no good,'
he said. 'I'm simply too upset to eat a single crumb.'

He gazed out of the porthole, but after ten minutes of
seeing nothing expect swirling grey, flopped back lifelessly
into his seat; remembering something he sat up straight
again.

'I wonder what happened to Luddite?' he said. 'Not that
I want him here with us—Grandmama's airship is the last
place I'd like a gremlin on the loose.'

'Umm . . . ?' Kit, seated at a little writing desk in the
corner, paused for a moment. 'I did ask Tita about him.
She said he was last seen heading towards the guild of
cuckoo clock makers, so that'll give 'em a nasty shock. I
'spect they'll have to change their name once he gets done
with 'em. I 'spect they'll have to call themselves the guild
of jigsaw makers from now on.'

Henry laughed then turned right round to see what Kit
was doing. There was a quill in his hand and his tongue
hung from the corner of his mouth giving him the
appearance of laboured concentration.

'What on earth are you writing?' asked Henry and he
got up to peer over Kit's shoulder, reading aloud, ' *"True
enchanters control the wind, only mindless children huff and
puff"* .'

Kit carried on writing despite a blot or two of ink mysteriously appearing on the paper. 'If we're going back to England I'll have to get these done for Mr O'Gloaming,' he explained, adding darkly, 'Teachers and elephants don't never forget.'

'That's not fair,' said Henry indignantly. 'Can't you explain to this Mr O'Gloaming that you've been rather busy recently? You stopped a war, you saved a country, you rescued a king, and you helped lift the good name of magic from the mud . . . hmm. It does sound a bit far-fetched when you say it out loud, doesn't it?'

'Very,' said Kit. 'As far-fetched as *a dragon ate my homework*. But don't you worry, Henry, I've only another six hundred and ninety-three more lines to go. With any luck I'll be finished by the time we reach London.'

# Other books by Stephen Elboz

## A Handful of Magic
ISBN 0 19 275134 4

*Suddenly Henry seemed to buckle at the knees. He let out a gasp of horror and his eyes jerked fully open. And snatching desperately at the air he slowly tipped backwards into the werewolves' den.*

Kit, son of the Queen's witch doctor, takes his best friend, Prince Henry, on a night time adventure to see the werewolves at the Tower of London. Henry falls into the den and is bitten, causing a rift between the Queen and Kit's father. The Queen sends for Stafford Sparks, the Royal Superintendent of Scientific Progress, to cure Henry, declaring that magic is dead and that electricity is the power of the future.

Kit is sent to live with his Aunt Pearl in her weird home on the tower of old St Paul's cathedral, but he is determined to save Henry from the clutches of Stafford Sparks and his electric shock treatment and prove that magic is still alive. But Kit's attempts to help his friend lead him into terrible danger in the tunnels under London, danger which even magic may not be able to overcome.

'A handful of magic? No, an entire universe of it. This book is sheer bliss.'
>           *The Guardian*

**The Tower at Moonville**

ISBN 0 19 275093 3

Moonville is a very strange school—there are no lessons and the boys are left to run riot. On the run from his wicked uncle, Nathan wonders what kind of mad world he has stumbled into.

He takes refuge in the tower with the mysterious scientist who lives there. But he can't hide away for ever and when his uncle finally catches up with him, Nathan finds himself in great danger . . .

'Nathan's adventures move at a hectic pace, and there's never a dull moment. This book will be greatly enjoyed.'

*Times Educational Supplement*

**Ghostlands**
ISBN 0 19 275092 5

From the moment Ewan steps through the door of the house, he realizes that this will be no ordinary visit. For one thing, Ziggy lives there—and Ziggy's a ghost. And where there's one ghost, there are bound to be others . . .

Ziggy and his ghoulish friends are in terrible danger. The local ghost-nappers are out to trap them and are not above a spot of devious magic to get what they want. And what has the theme park, Ghostlands, got to do with all this . . . ?

**The House of Rats**
ISBN 0 19 275021 6

Winner of the Smarties Young Judges Prize

The great house has become a dangerous place since the master mysteriously vanished. Wolves prowl around in the snow outside, hungry and howling, while inside the house, the horrible Aphid Dunn has taken charge. Everything seems to be falling apart.

Esther and the boys are wondering if things can get any worse, when they discover a whole new world under the house. There might still be one last chance at freedom after all . . .

'a brilliant story which grips you from the first to last page . . . *very* exciting.'
            *Mail on Sunday*

**A Store of Secrets**
ISBN 0 19 275067 4

Bridie can't understand it. Has Gramps vanished into thin air?
And what are the peculiar Crickbone twins doing in his yard?

All alone in the city, Bridie stumbles across the Byzantium
Bazaar, a crumbling department store crammed with cats and
cobwebs. And as she tries to discover the truth behind
Gramps's mysterious disappearance, other deeply held secrets
slowly begin to emerge . . .

'Elboz's imagination runs naturally to the baroque; it will be
fascinating to see where it takes him next.'
*Daily Telegraph*

## Temmi and the Flying Bears
ISBN 0 19 275015 1

Temmi is furious when the Witch-Queen's soldiers come to the village to steal one of the flying bears—even more so when he discovers that they've taken Cush, the youngest cub, who is Temmi's favourite bear. Temmi is determined to rescue Cush, but instead finds himself captured and taken to the Ice Castle where he will be a prisoner, too. Escape seems impossible—unless Temmi can somehow win over the ice-hearted Queen . . .

'You can almost feel the cold in this beautifully written, atmospheric and convincing fantasy, enthralling to the very end.'
    *Mail on Sunday*